1 THE DARING DECEPTION
2 NO DARKNESS FOR LOVE
3 THE LITTLE ADVENTURE
4 LESSONS IN LOVE
5 JOURNEY TO PARADISE
6 THE BORED BRIDEGROOM
7 THE PENNILESS PEER
8 THE DANGEROUS DANDY
9 THE RUTHLESS RAKE
10 THE WICKED MARQUIS
11 THE CASTLE OF FEAR
12 THE GLITTERING LIGHTS
13 A SWORD TO THE HEART
14 THE KARMA OF LOVE
15 THE MAGNIFICENT
   MARRIAGE
16 BEWITCHED
17 THE IMPETUOUS
   DUCHESS
18 THE FRIGHTENED BRIDE
19 THE SHADOW OF SIN
20 THE FLAME IS LOVE
21 THE TEARS OF LOVE
22 A VERY NAUGHTY ANGEL
23 CALL OF THE HEART
24 THE DEVIL IN LOVE
25 AS EAGLES FLY
26 LOVE IS INNOCENT
27 SAY YES, SAMANTHA
28 THE CRUEL COUNT
29 THE MASK OF LOVE
30 FIRE ON THE SNOW
31 AN ARROW OF LOVE
32 A GAMBLE WITH HEARTS

33 A KISS FOR THE KING
34 A FRAME OF DREAMS
35 THE FRAGRANT FLOWER
36 THE ELUSIVE EARL
37 MOON OVER EDEN
38 THE GOLDEN ILLUSION
39 THE HUSBAND HUNTERS
40 NO TIME FOR LOVE
41 PASSIONS IN THE SAND
42 THE SLAVES OF LOVE
43 AN ANGEL IN HELL
44 THE WILD CRY OF LOVE
45 THE BLUE-EYED WITCH
46 THE INCREDIBLE
   HONEYMOON
47 A DREAM FROM THE
   NIGHT
48 CONQUERED BY LOVE
49 NEVER LAUGH AT LOVE
50 THE SECRET OF THE
   GLEN
51 THE PROUD PRINCESS
52 HUNGRY FOR LOVE
53 THE HEART TRIUMPHANT
54 THE DREAM AND THE
   GLORY
55 THE TAMING OF LADY
   LORINDA
56 THE DISGRACEFUL DUKE
57 VOTE FOR LOVE
58 THE MYSTERIOUS MAID-
   SERVANT
59 THE MAGIC OF LOVE

Barbara Cartland's Library of Love

1 THE SHEIK
2 HIS HOUR

3 THE KNAVE OF DIAMONDS
4 A SAFETY MATCH

Barbara Cartland's Library of Love

THE SHEIK
BY E. M. HULL

CONDENSED BY
BARBARA CARTLAND

THE SHEIK
A Bantam Book / March 1977

ISBN 0-553-10497-7

Published simultaneously in the United States and Canada

Bantam Books are published by Bantam Books, Inc. Its trade-
mark, consisting of the words "Bantam Books" and the por-
trayal of a bantam, is registered in the United States Patent
Office and in other countries. Marca Registrada, Bantam
Books, Inc., 666 Fifth Avenue, New York, New York 10019.

Preface
by
Barbara Cartland

When *The Sheik* first appeared in 1921 we were stunned. This was the type of story we had never read before and it broke all the previous rules of story-telling.

Then the whole world became fascinated by the romance and allurement of the handsome, brutal, passionate Sheik, and he became the vogue. Even before he was portrayed on the Screen by the most glamorous film-star of the period, Rudolf Valentino, we had irretrievably lost our hearts to him.

We all saw ourselves in the role of Diana Mayo, we all longed to be abducted into the desert and to be forced by sheer violence into obedience by an all-conquering male.

Today the magic appeal of *The Sheik* is for me still there. I can only hope you will find it as captivating as I found it fifty-five years ago, and dream of a desert lover.

Chapter
One

"Are you coming to watch the dancing, Lady Conway?"

"I most decidedly am not. I thoroughly disapprove of the expedition of which this dance is the inauguration."

Lady Conway's voice became more positive as she continued:

"I consider that even by contemplating such a tour alone into the desert with no chaperon but with only native camel drivers and servants, Diana Mayo is behaving with a recklessness and impropriety that is calculated to cast a slur not only on her own reputation, but also on the prestige of her country. I blush to think of it."

She put her hand up to her cheek before she went on:

"We English cannot be too careful of our behaviour abroad. No opportunity is slight enough for our continental neighbours to cast stones, and this opportunity is very far from being slight. It is the maddest piece of unprincipled folly."

"Oh, come, Lady Conway! It's not quite as bad as all that. It is certainly unconventional and probably not quite wise, but remembering Miss Mayo's unusual upbringing . . ."

"I am not forgetting her unusual upbringing," interrupted Lady Conway. "It has been deplorable."

Drawing her wrap round her with a little shudder, Lady Conway stalked majestically across the wide verandah of the Biskra Hotel.

The two men left standing by the open French window that led into the hotel ballroom looked at each other and smiled.

"Some peroration," said one with a marked American accent. "That's the way scandal's made, I guess."

"Scandal be hanged! There's never been a breath of scandal attached to Diana Mayo's name. I've known the child since she was a baby. Confound that old woman! She would wreck the reputation of the Archangel Gabriel if he came down to earth, let alone that of a mere human girl."

"Not a very human girl," laughed the American. "She was sure meant for a boy and changed at the last moment. She looks like a boy in petticoats, a damned pretty boy—and a damned haughty one."

The Englishman laughed.

"There is a queer streak in the family, isn't there? Father was mad and blew his brains out, so I was told."

The Englishman shrugged his shoulders.

"You can call it mad, if you like," he said slowly. "I live near the Mayos in England, and happen to know the story. Sir John Mayo was passionately devoted to his wife; after twenty years of married life they were still lovers.

"Then this girl was born, the mother died. Two hours afterwards her husband shot himself, leaving the baby in the sole care of her brother, who was just nineteen, and as lazy and as selfish then as he is now.

"The problem of bringing up a girl child was too much trouble to be solved, so he settled the difficulty by treating her as if she were a boy. The result is what you see."

They moved nearer to the open window, looking into the brilliantly lit ballroom.

On a slightly raised platform at one end of the

room the host and hostess were receiving their guests. The brother and sister were singularly unlike. Sir Aubrey Mayo was very tall and thin.

The girl at his side appeared vividly alive. She was very slender, standing erect with the easy, vigorous carriage of an athletic boy, her small head poised proudly.

Her deep blue eyes were unusually clear and steady. The long, curling black lashes that shaded her eyes and the dark eyebrows were a foil to the thick crop of loose, red-gold curls that she wore short, clubbed about her ears.

"The result is worth seeing," said the American admiringly, referring to his companion's last remark.

A third and younger man joined them.

"Hallo, Arbuthnot. You're late. The divinity is ten deep in would-be partners already."

A dull red crept into the young man's face, and he jerked his head angrily.

"I got waylaid by Lady Conway—poisonous old woman! She had a great deal to say on the subject of Miss Mayo and her trip."

His eyes turned rather eagerly towards the end of the room where the girl was now standing alone. The American pushed Arbuthnot forward with a little laugh.

"Run along, foolish moth, and get your poor little wings singed."

Arbuthnot went through the window and worked slowly round the room. He came at last to the raised dais on which Diana Mayo was still standing, and climbed up the few steps to her side.

"This is luck, Miss Mayo," he said, with an assurance that he was far from feeling. "Am I really fortunate enough to find you without a partner?"

She turned to him slowly, with a little crease growing between her arched eyebrows, as if his coming were inopportune and she resented the interruption to her thoughts, and then she smiled quite frankly.

"I said I would not dance until everybody else was," she said rather doubtfully, looking about the crowded floor.

"They are all dancing. You've done your duty nobly. Don't miss this ripping tune," he urged persuasively.

She hesitated, tapping her programme-pencil against her teeth.

"I refused a lot of men," she said with a grimace, then she laughed. "Come along then. I am noted for my bad manners. This will only be one extra sin."

Arbuthnot danced well, but with the girl in his arms he seemed suddenly tongue-tied. They swung round the room several times, then halted simultaneously beside an open window and went out into the garden of the hotel, sitting down on a wicker seat under a gaudy Japanese hanging lantern.

The band was still playing, and for the moment the garden was empty, lit faintly by coloured lanterns, festooned by the palm trees, and twinkling lights outlining the winding paths.

Arbuthnot leaned forward, his hands clasped between his knees.

"I think you are the most perfect dancer I have ever met," he said a little breathlessly.

Miss Mayo looked at him seriously without a trace of self-consciousness.

"It is very easy to dance if you have a musical ear," she answered calmly.

"It's rather jolly here in the garden," Arbuthnot said tentatively.

His heart was pounding with unusual rapidity, and his eyes, which he kept fixed on his own clasped hands, had a hungry look growing in them.

"You mean that you want to sit out this dance with me?" she said with a boyish directness that somewhat nonplussed him.

"Yes," he stammered rather foolishly.

She held her programme up to the light of the lantern.

"I promised this one to Arthur Conway. We quarrel every time we meet. I cannot think why he asked me; he disapproves of me even more than his mother does. Anyway, I don't want to dance tonight. I am looking forward so tremendously to tomorrow."

"Are you really determined to go through with this trip?" he asked.

She stared at him in surprise.

"Why not? My arrangements have been made

6

for some time. Why should I change my mind at the last moment?"

"Why does your brother let you go alone? Why doesn't he go with you? Oh. I haven't any right to ask."

She shrugged her shoulders with a little laugh.

"We fell out, Aubrey and I. He wanted to go to America. I wanted a trip into the desert. We quarrelled and then we compromised. I shall have my desert tour, and Aubrey should go to New York.

"To mark his brotherly appreciation of my gracious promise to follow him to the States without fail at the end of a month, he has consented to grace my caravan for the first stage, and dismiss me on my way with his blessing."

"It isn't safe," Arbuthnot replied.

"I don't agree with you. I don't know why everybody is making such a fuss about it."

He looked at her curiously. She seemed to be totally unaware that it was her youth and her beauty that made all the danger of the expedition. He fell back on the easier excuse.

"There seems to be unrest amongst some of the tribes. There have been a lot of rumours lately."

She made a little movement of impatience.

"That's what they always tell you when they want to put obstacles in your way. The authorities have already dangled that bogey in front of me. I asked for facts and they only gave me generalities.

"I don't believe a word about the tribes being restless. Arabs are always moving about, aren't they? I have an excellent caravan leader, whom even the authorities vouch for, and I shall be armed.

"I am perfectly able to take care of myself. I can shoot straight and I am used to camping. Besides, I have given my word to Aubrey to be in Oran in a month, and I can't get very far away in that time."

There was an obstinate ring in her voice.

"Miss Mayo—Diana—put off this trip only for a little, and give me the right to go with you. I love you. I want you for my wife more than anything on earth. My God, Diana! Beauty like yours drives a man mad!"

"Is beauty all that a man wants in his wife?" she asked, with a kind of cold wonder in her voice. "Brains and a sound body seem much more sensible requirements to me."

"But when a woman has all three, as you have, Diana . . ." he whispered ardently, his hands closing over the slim ones lying in her lap.

But with a strength that seemed impossible for their smallness she disengaged them from his grasp.

"Please stop. I am sorry. We have been good friends, and it has never occurred to me that there could be anything beyond that. I never thought that you might love me. When God made me He omitted to give me a heart. I have never loved anyone in my life."

Arbuthnot sat in silence, and then he said quietly, "May I still be your friend, Diana?"

She looked at him a moment.

"Gladly," she said candidly. "I have hosts of acquaintances, but very few friends."

He held her slender fingers gripped in his for a moment, smothering an insane desire to press them to his lips, which he knew would be fatal to the newly accorded friendship, and then let them go.

Miss Mayo continued sitting quietly beside him.

And as they sat silently, her thoughts far away in the desert, a man's low voice rose in the stillness of the night.

"Pale hands I loved beside the Shalimar. Where are you now? Who lies beneath your spell?" he sang in a passionate, vibrating baritone.

He was singing in English, and the voice seemed to come from the dark shadows at the end of the garden.

He sang slowly, his voice lingering caressingly on the words, the last verse dying away softly and clearly, almost imperceptibly fading into silence.

For a moment there was utter stillness, then Diana lay back with a little sigh.

"The Kashmiri Song! It makes me think of India. I heard a man sing it in Kashmir last year, but not like that. What a wonderful voice! I wonder who it is."

Arbuthnot looked at her curiously, surprised at the sudden ring of interest in her tone and the sudden animation of her face.

"You say you have no emotion in your nature, and yet that unknown man's singing has stirred you deeply. How do you reconcile the two?" he asked almost angrily.

"Is an appreciation of the beautiful an emotion?" she challenged, with uplifted eyes. "Surely not. Music, art, nature, everything beautiful appeals to me."

She rose with a little laugh of pleasure.

Arbuthnot got up reluctantly and stood silent beside her for a few moments.

"Diana, I wish you'd let me kiss you, just once," he pleaded miserably.

She looked up swiftly with a glint of anger in her eyes, and shook her head.

"No. I have never been kissed in my life. It is one of the things that I do not understand."

Her voice was almost fierce.

She moved leisurely towards the hotel, and he walked beside her.

"Shall I see you in the morning?" she asked.

He understood. There was to be no more reference to what had passed between them.

"Yes. We have arranged an escort of about a dozen of us to ride the first few miles with you, to give you a proper send-off."

* * *

A few hours later Diana came into her bedroom. She stood in the middle of the room and looked at the preparations for the early start the next morning with a little smile of satisfaction.

Everything was *en train;* the final arrangements had all been concluded some days before.

The camel caravan with the camp equipment was due to leave Biskra a few hours before the time fixed for the Mayos to start with Mustafa Ali, the reputable guide whom the French authorities had reluctantly recommended.

The two big suitcases that Diana was taking with her stood open, already packed, waiting only for the last few necessaries, and by them the steamer trunk that Sir Aubrey would take charge of and leave in Paris as he passed through. On a chaise-longue was laid out her riding kit ready for the morning.

Her smile broadened as she looked at the smart-cut breeches and high brown boots. They were the clothes in which most of her life had been spent, and in which she was far more at home than in pretty dresses.

She crossed over to the dressing-table and looked at herself with a tinge of curiosity.

"I wonder why I'm so especially happy to-night."

She laughed again and undressed slowly and each moment felt more wide awake. Slipping a thin wrap over her pyjamas, she went out onto the broad balcony.

The room was on the first floor, and opposite her window rose one of the ornately carved and bracketed pillars that supported the balcony, stretching up to the second storey above her head.

She looked down into the gardens below and leant far over the rail. She thought she caught a glimpse of white drapery.

She looked again, but this time there was nothing.

It was a wonderful night, silent except for the cicadas' monotonous chirping, mysterious with the inexplicable mystery that hangs always in the Oriental night.

The smells of the East rose up all round her; here, as at home, they seemed more perceptible by night than by day.

"It's been a splendid life," she murmured, "and tomorrow—today—begins the most perfect part of it."

She yawned and realised suddenly that she was desperately sleepy. She turned back into her room, and, flinging off her wrap, tumbled into bed and slept almost before her head was on the pillow.

It must have been about an hour later when she awoke, suddenly wide awake. She lay quite still. The room was flooded with moonlight, there was nothing to be seen, but she had the positive feeling that there was another presence in the room besides her own.

She had had a half-conscious vision in the moment of waking of a shadowy something that had seemed to fade away by the window.

As the actual reality of this thought pierced through the sleep that dulled her brain and became a concrete suggestion, she sprang out of her bed and ran onto the balcony. She leaned over the railing, listening intently, but she could see nothing and hear nothing.

Puzzled, she went back into her room and

turned on the lights. Nothing seemed to be missing; the suitcases had apparently not been tampered with. By the bedside the ivory-mounted revolver that she always carried was lying as she had placed it.

"It must have been a dream," she said doubtfully, "but it seemed very real. It looked tall and white and solid, and I *felt* it there."

She waited a moment or two, then shrugged her shoulders, turned out the lights, and got into bed.

In five minutes she was asleep again.

Chapter
Two

The promised send-off had been enthusiastic. The arrangements for the trip had been perfect; there had been no hitch anywhere. The guide, Mustafa Ali, appeared capable and efficient.

The day had been full of interest, and the

long, hot ride had for Diana been the height of physical enjoyment.

They had reached the oasis where the first night was to be passed to find the camp already established, tents pitched, and everything so orderly that Sir Aubrey could find nothing to criticise.

Diana glanced round her little travelling tent with complete content. The narrow camp cot, the tin bath, the little folding table, and her two suit-cases seemed to take up all the available space.

She had changed from her riding clothes into a dress of clinging jade-green silk, the neck cut low to reveal her white skin.

She came out of the tent, stood a moment, and drew a long breath.

It was the desert at last, the desert that she felt she had been longing for all her life.

She had never known until this moment how intense the longing had been. She felt strangely at home, as if the great, silent emptiness had been waiting for her as she had been waiting for it.

Her brother's voice behind her brought her down to earth suddenly.

"You've been a confounded long time."

She turned to the table with a faint smile.

"Don't be a bear, Aubrey. It's all very well for you. You have Stephens to lather your chin and to wash your hands, but I have to look after my-self."

"Are you going to rig yourself out like that every evening for the benefit of Mustafa Ali and the camel-drivers?" he asked.

"I do not propose to invite the worthy Mustafa to meals, and I am not in the habit of 'rigging myself out,' as you so charmingly put it, for anyone's benefit. If you think I dress in camp to please you, my dear Aubrey, you flatter yourself. I do it entirely to please myself.

"That explorer woman we met in London the first year I began travelling with you explained to me the real moral and physical value of changing into comfortable, pretty clothes after a hard day in breeches and boots. You change yourself. What's the difference?"

"All the difference," he snapped. "There is no need for you to make yourself more attractive than you are already."

"Since when has it occurred to you that I am attractive? You must have a touch of the sun, Aubrey," she replied.

"Don't quibble. You know perfectly well that you are good-looking—too good-looking to carry through this preposterous affair."

"What do you mean?" she asked.

"I've been doing some hard thinking today, Diana. This tour you propose is impossible."

"Isn't it rather late in the day to find that out?" she interrupted sarcastically.

"You must see for yourself," he went on, "that it's quite unthinkable that you can wander for the next month all alone in the desert.

"Though my legal guardianship over you terminated last September, I still have some moral obligations towards you. Though it has been convenient to me to bring you up as a boy and to regard you in the light of a younger brother instead of a sister, we cannot get away from the fact that you are a woman, and a very young woman."

Diana swung round on her chair with a hard laugh.

"If I had not lived with you all my life, Aubrey, I should really be impressed with your brotherly solicitude. But knowing you as I do, I know that it is not anxiety on my behalf that is prompting you, but the disinclination that you have to travel alone without me."

"Diana, give up this insane trip," he begged.

"I will not."

"I've a thundering good mind to make you."

"You can't. I'm my own mistress. You have no right over me at all. You have no claim on me. You haven't even that of ordinary brotherly affection. You have never given me any, so you cannot expect it from me. I am not going to argue any more. I will not go back to Biskra."

"Diana, listen to reason!"

"Aubrey! I have said my last word. Nothing will alter my determination to go on this trip."

They were facing each other across the little table. An angry flush rose in Sir Aubrey's face.

"You're a damned obstinate little devil!" he said furiously.

She looked at him steadily.

"I am what you have made me," she said slowly. "Why quarrel with the results? You have brought me up to ignore the restrictions attached to my sex; you now round on me and throw them in my face.

"You have made me as hard as yourself, and you now profess surprise at the determination your training has forced upon me.

"As I reminded you before, I am my own mistress, and I will submit to no interference with my actions. Please understand that clearly, Aubrey. I don't want to wrangle any more.

"I will join you in New York as I promised, but I will do what I choose, when and how I choose, and I will *never* obey any will but my own."

Sir Aubrey's eyes narrowed suddenly.

"Then I hope to heaven that one day you will fall into the hands of a man who will make you obey," he cried wrathfully.

* * *

She was almost aggressively cheerful the next morning at breakfast.

The time for starting came. Stephens was fussing about the horse that Diana was to ride.

"Everything all right, Stephens? Up to your standard? Don't look so glum. I wish you were coming to look after me, but it couldn't be done. Sir Aubrey would be lost without you."

The idea of a tour without Stephens in the background seemed suddenly momentous, and the smile she gave him was more serious than she meant it to be. She went back to her brother.

"I don't think there's any use waiting any

longer. You won't want to hurry yourself too much, and you will want to be in Biskra in time for dinner," she said as casually as she could.

He swung towards her.

"Diana, it's still not too late to change your mind. For heaven's sake give up this folly. It's tempting Providence."

For the first time there was a genuine ring in his voice, and for a moment Diana wavered, but only for a moment. Then she looked at him with a slow smile.

"Don't be ridiculous, Aubrey. You can't expect me to change my mind at the eleventh hour. It's perfectly safe. Mustafa Ali will take care that everything goes smoothly. He has his reputation in Biskra to think of.

"You know the character the authorities give him. He is not likely to throw that away. In any case I can take care of myself, thanks to your training. I don't mind owning to being conceited about my shooting. Even you admit that I am a credit to your teaching."

With a gay little laugh she whipped out the ivory-mounted revolver, and aiming at a low flat rock some distance away, fired.

She was an unusually good revolver shot, but this time she seemed to have missed. There was no mark on the stone.

Diana stared at it stupidly, a frown of perplexity creasing her forehead. Then she looked at her brother, and back to the revolver in her hand.

Sir Aubrey swore.

"Diana! What a senseless piece of bravado!" he cried angrily.

She took no notice of him. She was still staring at the smooth rock face.

"I don't understand it. How could I miss? It's as big as a house," she murmured thoughtfully, and raised the revolver again.

But Sir Aubrey caught her wrist.

"For God's sake don't make a fool of yourself a second time. You have lowered your prestige quite enough already," he said in a low voice, with a glance at the group of watching Arabs.

Diana jerked the little weapon back into its place reluctantly.

"I don't understand it," she said again. "It must be the light."

She mounted and wheeled her horse alongside Sir Aubrey's, and held out her hand.

"Good-bye, Aubrey. Expect me a month after you arrive. I will cable to you from Cherbourg. Good luck!"

With a nod to Mustafa Ali she turned her horse's head southwards.

For a long time she rode in silence. The quarrel with Aubrey had left a nasty taste in her mouth. She knew that what she was doing was considered unconventional, but she had been brought up to be unconventional.

There was nothing strange about the scene that lay all round her. Her surroundings seemed oddly familiar.

The burning sun overhead in the cloudless sky,

the shimmering haze rising from the hot, dry ground, and the feathery outline of some clustering palm trees in a tiny distant oasis were like remembrances that she watched again with a feeling of gladness that was fuller and deeper than anything that she had been conscious of before.

She was radiantly happy—happy in the sense of her youth and strength, her perfect physical fitness, happy in the capacity of her power of enjoyment, happy with the touch of the keen, nervous horse between her knees, exhilarated with her new authority.

A caravan that had been visible for a long time coming towards them drew nearer, and Diana reined in to watch the long line of slow, lurching camels passing.

The great beasts, with their disdainful tread and long, swaying necks, never failed to interest her. It was a large caravan; it took some time to pass.

One or two of the camels carried huddled figures, swathed and shapeless with a multitude of coverings, that Diana knew must be women. The contrast between them and herself was almost ridiculous. It made her feel stifled even to look at them.

She wondered what their lives were like, if they ever rebelled against the drudgery and restrictions that were imposed upon them, if they ever longed for the freedom that she was revelling in.

The thought of those lives filled her with aversion. The idea of marriage was repugnant to her.

She thought of it with a shiver of absolute repulsion.

That women could submit to the degrading intimacy and fettered existence of married life filled her with scornful wonder. To be bound irrevocably to the will and pleasure of a man who would have the right to demand obedience in all that constituted marriage and the strength to enforce those claims revolted her.

For a Western woman it was bad enough, but for the women of the East, mere slaves of the passions of the men who owned them, unconsidered, disregarded, reduced to the level of animals—the bare idea made her quiver and bring her hand down heavily on her horse's neck.

The nervous creature started sharply and she let him go, calling to Mustafa Ali as she cantered past him.

There was a look of annoyance on Mustafa Ali's face as she turned on hearing him behind her and signalled to him to ride beside her.

"*Mademoiselle* is not interested in the caravan?" he asked curiously.

"No," she replied shortly.

They continued on, and she asked Mustafa Ali about the country through which they were passing, but he did not seem to have much information that was really of interest.

The arrival at a little oasis where the guide suggested that the midday halt might be made was opportune. Diana swung to the ground, and, tossing down her gloves, gave herself a shake. It was hot work riding in the burning sun, and the rest would be delightful.

She had a thoroughly healthy appetite, and superintended the laying out of her lunch with interest. She finished quickly, and then, with her back propped against a palm tree, her arms clasped round her knees, she settled down happily, overlooking the desert.

Here she would be free from anything that could mar her perfect enjoyment of life as it appeared to her. Here there was nothing to spoil her pleasure.

It was the happiest day of her life. She had forgotten the quarrel with Aubrey. She had put from her mind the chain of ideas suggested by the passing caravan. There was nothing discordant to disturb the perfect harmony of her mind.

A shadow beside her made her turn her head. Mustafa Ali salaamed obsequiously.

"It is time to start, *Mademoiselle*."

Diana looked up in surprise and then back over her shoulder at the escort. The men were already mounted.

The smile faded from her eyes. Mustafa Ali was guide, but she was head of this expedition; if her guide had not realised this he would have to do so now. She glanced at the watch on her wrist.

"There is plenty of time," she said coolly.

Mustafa Ali salaamed again.

"It is a long ride to reach the oasis where we must camp tonight," he insisted.

"Then we can ride faster," she replied quietly.

Mustafa Ali made a movement of impatience and persisted doggedly.

"*Mademoiselle* would do well to start."

Diana looked up swiftly with angry eyes.

Under the man's suave manner and simple words a peremptory tone had crept into his voice. She sat quite still, and under her haughty stare the guide's eyes wavered and turned away.

"We will start when I choose, Mustafa Ali," she said brusquely. "You may give orders to your men, but you will take your orders from me. I will tell you when I am ready. You may go."

Still he hesitated, swaying irresolutely backwards and forwards on his heels.

Diana snapped her fingers over her shoulder, a trick she had learned from a French officer in Biskra.

"I said go!" she repeated sharply.

She did not look back to see what orders he gave the men. Perhaps it was growing late, perhaps the camp was a longer ride than she had thought; but Mustafa Ali must learn his lesson even if they had to ride till midnight to reach the oasis.

She pushed her obstinate chin out farther and then smiled again suddenly. She hoped that the night would fall before they reached their destination. There had been one or two moonlight riding picnics out from Biskra, and the glamour of the desert nights had gone to Diana's head.

This riding into the unknown, away from the noisy, chattering crowd who had spoiled the perfect stillness of the night, would be infinitely more perfect.

She gave a little sigh of regret as she thought of it. It was not really practical. Though she would wait nearly another hour to allow the fact of her authority to sink into Mustafa Ali's brain, she would have to hasten afterwards to arrive at the camp before darkness set in.

The men were unused to her ways and she to theirs. One hour would not make much difference. The horses could be pushed along a bit faster with no harm happening to them.

She eyed her watch from time to time with a grin of amusement, but suppressed the temptation to look and see how Mustafa Ali was taking it, for her action might be seen and misconstrued.

When the time she had set herself was up, she rose and walked slowly towards the group of Arabs. The guide's face was sullen, but taking no notice she mounted and rode forward steadily.

She had been quite right about the capabilities of the horses. They responded without any apparent effort to the further demand made of them. The one in particular that Diana was riding moved in a swift, easy gallop that was the perfection of motion.

They had been riding for some hours when they came to the first oasis that had been sighted since leaving the one where the midday halt was made. Diana pulled up her horse to look at it, for it was unusually beautiful in the luxuriousness and arrangement of its groups of palms and leafy bushes.

She took off her heavy helmet and tossed it to the man behind her, and sat looking at the oasis while the faint breeze that had sprung up stirred her thick, short hair and cooled her hot head.

She turned eagerly to Mustafa Ali.

"Why did you not arrange for the camp to be here? It would have been a long enough ride."

The man fidgeted in his saddle, fingering his beard uneasily, his eyes wandering past Diana's and looking at the broken trees.

"No man rests here, *Mademoiselle*. It is the place of devils. The curse of Allah is upon it," he muttered, touching his horse with his heel, and making it sidle restlessly—an obvious hint that Diana ignored.

"I like it," she persisted obstinately.

He made a quick gesture with his fingers.

"It is accursed. Death lurks beside those broken palm trees," he said, looking at her curiously.

She jerked her head with a sudden smile.

"For you perhaps, but not for me. Allah's curse rests only upon those who fear it. But since you are afraid, Mustafa Ali, let us go on."

She gave a little light laugh, and Mustafa Ali kicked his horse savagely as he followed.

She rode on until she began to wonder if it would indeed be nightfall before she reached her destination. They had ridden longer and faster than had ever been intended. It seemed odd that they had not overtaken the baggage camels. She looked at her watch with a frown.

"Where is your caravan, Mustafa Ali?" she called. "I see no sign of an oasis, and the darkness will soon come."

"If *Mademoiselle* had started earlier—" he said sullenly.

"If I had started earlier it would still have been too far. Tomorrow we will arrange it otherwise," she said firmly.

"Tomorrow—" he growled indistinctly.

Diana looked at him keenly.

"What did you say?" she asked haughtily.

His hand went to his forehead mechanically.

"Tomorrow is with Allah!" he murmured with unctuous piety.

A retort trembled on Diana's lips, but her attention was distracted from her annoying guide to a collection of black specks far off across the desert. They were too far away for her to see clearly, but she pointed to them, peering at them intently.

"See!" she cried. "Is that the caravan?"

"As Allah wills!" he replied more piously than before.

The black specks were moving fast across the level plain. Very soon Diana saw that it was not the slow, leisurely camels that they were overtaking, but a band of mounted men who were moving swiftly towards them.

They had seen nobody since the traders' caravan had passed them in the morning. For Diana, the Arabs that were approaching were even more interesting than the caravan had been.

She had seen plenty of caravans arriving at and departing from Biskra, but, though she had seen small parties of tribesmen constantly in the vicinity of the town, she had never seen so large a body of mounted men before, nor had she seen them as they were here, one with the wild picturesqueness of their surroundings.

It was impossible to count how many there were, for they were riding in close formation, the wind filling their great white cloaks, making each man look gigantic. Diana's interest flamed up excitedly.

It was like passing another ship upon a hitherto empty sea. They seemed to add a desired touch to the grim loneliness of the scene, which had begun to be a little awe inspiring.

The distance between the two parties decreased rapidly. Diana, intent on the quickly advancing horsemen, spurred ahead of her guide with sparkling eyes.

They were near enough now to see that the horses were beautiful creatures and that each man rode magnificently. They were armed too, their rifles being held in front of them, not slung on their backs as she had seen in Biskra.

They passed quite close to her, only a few yards away—a solid square, the orderly ranks suggesting training and discipline that she had not looked for. Not a head turned in her direction as they went by and the pace was not slackened.

Fretted by the proximity of the galloping horses, her own horse reared impatiently, but Diana pulled him in, turning in her saddle to watch the Arabs pass, her breath coming quickly with excitement.

"What are they?" she called out to Mustafa Ali, who had dropped some way behind her.

But he, too, was looking back at the horsemen, and did not seem to hear her question. Her escort had lagged still farther behind her guide, and were some little distance away. Diana watched the rapidly moving, compact square eagerly with appreciative eyes—it was a beautiful sight.

Then she gave a little gasp. The galloping horses had drawn level with the last stragglers of her own party, and just beyond them they stopped suddenly.

Diana would not have believed it possible that they could have stopped so suddenly and in such close formation while travelling at such a pace.

The tremendous strain on the bridles flung the horses far back on their haunches. But there was no time to dwell on the wonderful horsemanship or training of the men. Events moved too rapidly.

The solid square split up and lengthened out into a long line of men riding two abreast. Wheeling behind the last of Mustafa's men, they came back even faster than they had passed, and circled widely round Diana and her attendants.

Bewildered by this manoeuvre, she watched them with a puzzled frown, striving to soothe her horse, who was nearly frantic with excitement. Twice they galloped round her little band, their long white cloaks fluttering, their rifles tossing in their hands.

Diana was growing impatient. It was very fine to watch, but time and the light were both going. She would have been glad if the demonstration had occurred earlier in the day, when there would have been more time to enjoy it.

She turned again to Mustafa Ali to suggest that they had better try to move on, but he had gone farther from her, back towards his own men.

She wrestled with her nervous mount, trying to turn him to join her guide, when a sudden burst of rifle shots made her start and her horse bound violently. Then she laughed.

That would be the end of the demonstration, a parting salute, the *decharge de mousqueterie* beloved of the Arabs. She turned her head to look at them ride off, and the laugh died away on her lips.

It was not a farewell salute. The rifles that the Arabs were firing were not pointing up into the heavens, but aiming straight at her and her escort.

And as she stared with suddenly startled eyes, unable to do anything with her plunging horse, Mustafa Ali's men were blotted out from her sight, cut off by a band of Arabs who rode between her and them.

Then there came another volley, and she saw the guide slide slowly out of his saddle and onto the ground, and at the same time Diana's horse went off with a wild leap that nearly unseated her.

Until they started shooting, the thought that the Arabs could be hostile had not crossed her mind. She imagined that they were merely showing off with the childish love of display which she knew was characteristic of them.

For the first time it occurred to her that her guide's descent from his saddle was due to a wound and not to the fear that she had at first disgustedly attributed to him. But nobody seemed to put up any kind of a fight, she thought wrathfully.

She tugged angrily at her horse's mouth, but the bit was between his teeth and he tore on frantically. Her own position made her furious.

Her guide was wounded, his men surrounded, and she was ignominiously being run away with by a bolting horse.

Then as she hauled ineffectually at the bridle with all her strength there came from behind her the sound of a long, shrill whistle.

Her horse pricked up his ears and she was conscious that his pace sensibly lessened. Instinctively she looked behind.

A solitary Arab was riding after her, and as she looked she realised that his horse was gaining on hers. The thought drove from her every idea of stopping her runaway and made her dig her spurs into him instead.

There was a sinister air of deliberation in the way in which the Arab was following her; he was riding her down.

Diana's mouth closed firmly, and a new keenness came into her steady eyes. It was one thing to go back voluntarily to make terms with the men who had attacked her party; it was quite another thing to be deliberately chased across the desert by an Arab freebooter.

New experiences were crowding in upon her today. She had often wondered what the feelings of a hunted creature were.

She could ride, and there seemed plenty of speed yet in the frightened animal under her. She bent down, lying low against his neck with a little, reckless laugh, alternately coaxing him with all her knowledge and spurring him.

She frowned anxiously as she looked at the last rays of the setting sun. It would be dark very soon, but she would not give in. She would ride till she dropped, or the horse did.

The whistle came again, and again, in spite of her relentless spurring, her horse checked his pace. A sudden inspiration came to her.

Perhaps it was the horse she was riding that was the cause of all the trouble. It was certainly the Arab's whistle that had made it moderate its speed; it was responding clearly to a signal that it knew.

Her guide's reluctance to give any particulars of his acquisition of the horse came back to her. The animal had unquestionably been stolen, and either belonged to or was known to the party of Arabs who had met them.

She urged the horse on with all her power, but he was slowing up perceptibly. She flashed another backwards look. The Arab was close behind her—closer than she had been aware.

She had a momentary glimpse of a big white figure, dark piercing eyes and white gleaming teeth; and passionate rage filled her.

With no thought of what the consequences or retaliation might be, with no thought at all beyond a wild desire to rid herself of her pursuer, driven by a sudden madness which seemed to rise up in her and which she could not control, she clutched her revolver.

She fired twice, full in the face of the man who was following her. He did not even flinch, and a low laugh of amusement came from him.

And at the sound of his laugh Diana's mouth parched suddenly, and a little cold shiver rippled across her spine. A strange feeling that she had never experienced before went through her.

She had missed again as she had missed this morning. How, she did not know; it was inexplicable, but it was a fact, and a fact that left her with a feeling of powerlessness.

She dropped the useless revolver, trying vainly to force her horse's pace, but inch by inch the fiery chestnut that the Arab was riding crept up nearer alongside.

She would not turn to look again, but glancing sideways she could see its small, wicked-looking head, with flat-laid ears and vicious, bloodshot eyes, level with her elbow.

Then with a sudden spurt the chestnut forged ahead, and as it shot past it swerved close in beside her, and the man, rising in his stirrups and leaning towards her, flung a pair of powerful arms round her.

With a jerk he swung her clear of the saddle and onto his own horse in front of him. His movement had been so quick that she had been unprepared and unable to resist.

For a moment she was stunned, then her senses came back to her and she struggled wildly.

But she was stifled in the thick folds of the Arab's robes, against which her face was crushed, and held in a grip that seemed to be slowly suffocating her, and her struggles were futile.

The hard, muscular arm round her hurt her acutely, her ribs seemed to be almost breaking under its weight and strength, and it was nearly impossible to breathe with the close contact of his body.

She was unusually strong for a girl, but against this steely strength that held her she was helpless.

Her feelings were indescribable. She did not know what to think. Her mind felt jarred. She was unable to frame any thought coherently. What had happened was so unexpected, so preposterous, that no conclusion seemed adequate.

Only rage filled her—blind, passionate rage against the man who had dared to touch her, who had dared to lay his hands on her.

A shiver of revulsion ran through her. She was choking with fury, with anger, and with disgust. The ignominy of her plight hurt her pride badly.

She had been outridden, swept from her saddle as if she were a puppet, and compelled to bear the proximity of the man's own hateful body and the restraint of his arms.

No one had ever dared to touch her before. No one had ever dared to handle her as she was being handled now. How was it going to end? Where were they going? With her face hidden she had lost all sense of direction.

The fresh strength that the air gave her fanned the courage that still remained with her. Collecting all her force, she made a sudden desperate spring, her spurred heels tearing the chestnut's flank until he reared perpendicularly, snorting and trembling.

But with a quick sweep of his long arm the Arab gathered her back into his hold, still struggling fiercely. Both his arms were round her; he was controlling the maddened horse only with the pressure of his knees.

"Doucement, doucement."

She heard the slow, soft voice indistinctly, for he was pressing her head closely to him, and she did not know if the words were applied to herself or to the horse.

She fought to lift her head, to escape the grip that held her, straining, striving, until he spoke again.

"Lie still, you little fool!" he snarled with sudden vehemence.

With brutal hands he forced her to obey him, until she wondered if he would leave a single bone unbroken in her body, till further resistance was impossible. Gasping for breath, she yielded to the strength that overpowered her, and ceased to struggle.

The man seemed to know intuitively that she was beaten, and turned his undivided attention to his horse with the same low laugh of amusement that had sent the strange feeling through her when her shots had missed him.

It had puzzled her then, but it grew now with a horrible intensity, until she knew that it was fear that had come to her for the first time in her life.

A strange fear that she fought against desperately, but which was gaining on her with a force that was sapping her strength from her and making her head reel.

She did not faint, but her whole body seemed to grow nerveless with the sudden realisation of the horror of her position.

The Arab moved her position once, roughly, but she was glad of the change, for it freed her head from the stifling folds of his robes. He did not speak again—only once when the chestnut shied violently he muttered something under his breath. But her satisfaction was short-lived.

A few minutes afterwards his arm tightened round her once more and he twined a fold of his long cloak round her head, blinding her. And then she understood.

The galloping horse was pulled in with almost the same suddenness that had amazed her when she had first seen the Arabs.

She felt him draw her close into his arms and

slip down onto the ground; there were voices round her—confused, unintelligible; then they died away as she felt him carry her a few paces.

He set her down and unwound the covering from her face. The light that shone round her seemed dazzling by contrast with the darkness that had gone before. Confused, she clasped her hands over her eyes for a moment and then looked up slowly.

She was in a big, lofty tent, brightly lit by two hanging lamps. But she took no heed of her surroundings; her eyes were fixed on the man who had brought her there.

He had flung aside the heavy cloak that enveloped him from head to foot, and was standing before her, tall and broad-shouldered.

He was dressed in white flowing robes, a waist-cloth embroidered in black and silver wound several times about him, from the top of which showed a revolver that was thrust into the folds.

Diana's eyes passed over him slowly till they rested on his brown, clean-shaven face, surmounted by crisp, close-cut brown hair. It was the handsomest and the cruelest face that she had ever seen.

Her gaze was drawn instinctively to his. He was looking at her with fierce burning eyes that swept her until she felt that the boyish clothes that covered her slender limbs were stripped from her, leaving the beautiful white body bare under his passionate stare.

She shrank back, quivering, dragging the lapels of her riding jacket together over her breast with clutching hands, obeying an impulse that she hardly understood.

"Who are you?" she gasped hoarsely.

"I am the Sheik Ahmed Ben Hassan."

The name conveyed nothing. She had never heard it before. Without thinking, she had spoken in French, and in French he replied to her.

"Why have you brought me here?" she asked, fighting down the fear that was growing more terrible every moment.

He repeated her words with a slow smile.

"Why have I brought you here? *Bon Dieu!* Are you not woman enough to know?"

She shrank back farther, a wave of colour rushing into her face, then receded immediately, leaving her whiter than she had been before. Her eyes fell under the kindling flame in his.

"I don't know what you mean," she whispered faintly, with shaking lips.

"I think you do."

He laughed softly, and his laugh frightened her more than anything he had said.

He came towards her, and although she was swaying on her feet, desperately she tried to evade him, but with a quick movement he caught her in his arms.

Terror, agonising, soul-shaking terror such as she had never imagined, took hold of her.

The flaming light of desire burning in his eyes turned her sick and faint. Her body throbbed with the consciousness of a knowledge that appalled her.

She understood his purpose with a horror that

made each separate nerve in her system shrink against the understanding that had come to her in the consuming fire of his ardent gaze, and in the fierce embrace that was drawing her shaking limbs closer and closer against the man's own pulsating body.

She writhed in his arms as he crushed her to him in a sudden excess of possessive passion. His head bent slowly down to her, his eyes burned deeper, and, held immovable, she endured the first kiss she had ever received.

And the touch of his scorching lips, the clasp of his arms, and the close union with his warm, strong body robbed her of all strength, of all power of resistance.

With a great sob her eyes closed wearily, and the hot mouth pressed on hers was like a narcotic, drugging her almost into insensibility.

Numbly she felt him gather her high up into his arms, his lips still clinging closely, and carry her across the tent and through curtains into an adjoining room. He laid her down on soft cushions.

"Do not make me wait too long," he whispered, and left her.

The whispered words sent a shock through her that seemed to wrench her deadened nerves apart, galvanising her into sudden strength. She sprang up with wild, despairing eyes, and hands clenched frantically across her heavy breast.

Then with a bitter cry she dropped onto the floor, her arms flung up and out across the wide, luxurious bed. It was not true! It was not true! It could not be—this awful thing that had happened to her—not to her, Diana Mayo!

It was a dream, a ghastly dream that would pass and free her from this agony.

Shuddering, she raised her head. The strange room swam before her eyes. Oh, God! It was not a dream. It was real, it was an actual fact from which there was no escape.

She was trapped, powerless, defenceless, and behind the heavy curtains near her was the man waiting to claim what he had taken. Any moment he might come.

The thought sent her shivering closer to the ground with limbs that trembled uncontrollably.

Her courage, which had faced dangers and even death without flinching, broke down before the horror that awaited her. It was inevitable; there was no help to be expected, no mercy to be hoped for. She had felt the crushing strength against which she was helpless.

She would struggle, but it would be useless; she would fight, but it would make no difference. Within the tent she was alone, ready to his hand like a snared animal; without, the place was swarming with the man's followers.

There was nowhere she could turn, there was no one she could turn to. The certainty of the accomplishment of what she dreaded crushed her with its surety. All power of action was gone.

She could only wait and suffer in the complete moral collapse that overwhelmed her, and that was rendered greater by her temperament.

Her body was aching with the grip of his powerful arms, her mouth was bruised with his savage kisses. She clenched her hands in anguish.

"O, God!" she sobbed, with scalding tears that scorched her cheeks. "Curse him! Curse him!"

And with the words on her lips he came, silent, noiseless, to her side.

His eyes were fierce, his stern mouth parted in a cruel smile, his deep, slow voice half angry, half impatiently amused.

"Must I be valet as well as lover?"

Chapter
Three

The warm sunshine was flooding the tent when Diana awoke from the deep sleep of exhaustion that had been almost insensibility, awoke to immediate and complete remembrance.

One quick, fearful glance round the big room

assured her that she was alone. She sat up slowly, her eyes shadowy with pain, looking listlessly at the luxurious appointments of the tent.

She was dry-eyed; she had no tears left. They had all been expended when she had grovelled at his feet, imploring the mercy he had not accorded her.

She had fought until the unequal struggle had left her exhausted and helpless in his arms, until her whole body was one agonised ache from the brutal hands that forced her into compliance.

She had fought until her courageous spirit was crushed by the realisation of her own powerlessness, and by the strange fear that the man himself awakened in her, which had driven her at last moaning to her knees.

The recollection of her abject prayers and weeping supplications filled her with a burning shame. She loathed herself with bitter contempt.

Her courage had broken down; even her pride had failed her.

She wound her arms about her knees and hid her face against them.

"Coward! Coward!" she whispered fiercely.

Why had she not scorned him? Or why had she not suffered in silence all that he had done to her?

It would have pleased him less than the frenzied entreaties that had only provoked the soft laugh that made her shiver each time she heard it.

She shivered now.

"I thought I was brave," she murmured brokenly. "I am only a coward, a craven."

She lifted her head at last and looked round her. The room was a curious mixture of Oriental luxury and European comfort. The lavish sumptuousness of the furnishings suggested subtly an unrestrained indulgence; the whole atmosphere was voluptuous.

There was nothing that jarred artistically, the rich hangings all harmonised, there were no glaring incongruities such as she had seen in native palaces in India.

And everything on which her eyes rested drove home relentlessly the hideous fact of her position.

His things were everywhere. On a low, brass-topped table by the bed was the half-smoked Turkish cigarette he had had between his lips when he came to her. The pillow beside her still bore the impress of his head.

She looked at it with a growing horror in her eyes until an uncontrollable shuddering seized her and she cowered down, smothering the cry that burst from her in the soft pillow and dragging the silken coverings up round her as if their thin shelter were a protection.

She lived again through every moment of the past night until thought was unendurable, until she felt that she would go mad, until at last, worn out, she fell asleep.

It was midday when she awoke again.

This time she was not alone. A young Arab girl was sitting on the rug beside her, looking at her with soft brown eyes of absorbed interest.

As Diana sat up the girl rose to her feet, salaaming with a timid smile.

"I am Zilah, to wait on *Madame*," she said shyly in stumbling French, holding out a wrap that Diana recognised with wonder as her own.

She looked behind her. Her suitcases were lying near her, open, partially unpacked. The missing baggage camels had been captured first, then.

She was at least to be allowed the use of her own belongings. A gleam of anger shot into her tired eyes and she swung round with a sharp question.

But the Arab girl shook her head uncomprehendingly, drawing back with frightened eyes; and to all further questions she remained silent, with down-dropping mouth like that of a scared child.

She evidently only half understood what was said to her and could give no answer to what she did understand, and turned away with obvious relief when Diana stopped speaking.

She went across the tent and pulled aside a curtain leading into a bathroom that was as big and far better equipped than the one that Diana had had in the Indian tent, and which, up to now, had seemed the last word in comfort and luxury.

Though the girl's knowledge of French was limited, her hands were deft enough, but her ignorance of the intricacies of a European woman's *toilette* was very apparent, and constantly provoked in her a girlish giggle that changed hurriedly to a startled gravity when Diana looked at her.

Laughter was very far from Diana, but she could not help smiling now and again at her funny mistakes.

The girl, with her big, wondering eyes, her shy, hesitating French and childish curiosity, in some indefinable way gave back to Diana the self-control that had slipped from her.

The hot bath that took the soreness out of her limbs brought back the colour to her face and lips.

She even washed her hair, rubbing the glistening curls dry with fierce vigour, striving to rid herself of the contamination that seemed to have saturated her.

Yet the robes against which they had been pressed were spotless, and the hands that had held her were fastidiously clean, even to the well-kept nails.

She came back into the bedroom to find Zilah on her knees, poring over her wardrobe with bewilderment, fingering the evening dresses with shy hands, and finally submitting tentatively to Diana the tweed skirt that had been packed with her other things for the journey after Oran should be reached.

But Diana put it aside, and pointed to the riding clothes she had worn the previous day.

In them she felt more able to face what might be before her, the associations connected with them seemed to give her moral strength, in them she would feel herself again—Diana the boy, not the shivering piece of womanhood that had been born with tears and agony last night.

She bit her lip as she stamped her foot down into the long boot.

She sent the girl away at last, and noticed that she avoided passing into the adjoining room, but vanished instead through the curtains leading into the bathroom.

Did that mean that in the outer room the Arab Sheik was waiting? The thought banished the self-control she had regained and sent her weakly onto the side of the bed with her face hidden in her hands.

Was he there?

Her questions to the little waiting-girl had only been concerned with the whereabouts of the camp to which she had been brought and also with the fate of the caravan; of the man himself she had not been able to bring herself to speak.

The thought of seeing him again brought a shame that was unspeakable. But she conquered the agitation that threatened to grow beyond restraint, pride helping her again.

It was better to face the inevitability of her own free will than be fetched whether she would or not.

She knew now the strength of the man who had abducted her, knew that physically she was helpless against him.

She raised her head and listened. It was very silent in the next room. Perhaps she was to be allowed a further respite. She jerked her head impatiently at her own hesitation.

"Coward!" she whispered again contemptuously, and flung across the room.

But at the curtains she halted for a moment, then with set face drew them aside and went through.

The respite had been granted; the room appeared to be empty.

But as she crossed the thick rugs her heart leapt suddenly into her throat, for she became aware of a man standing in the open doorway.

His back was turned to her, but in a moment she saw that the short, slim figure in white linen European clothes bore no resemblance to the tall Arab she had expected to see.

She thought her footsteps were noiseless, but he turned with a little quick bow. A typical Frenchman with narrow, clean-shaven face, sleek black hair, dark restless eyes, and the manners of a well-trained servant.

Diana coloured hotly under his glance, but his eyes were lowered instantly.

"*Madame* is doubtless ready for lunch."

His movements were as quick and as quiet as his voice, and as if in a dream Diana found herself in a few moments before a lunch that was perfectly cooked and daintily served.

The man hovered about her solicitously, attending to her wants with dexterous hands and watchful eyes that anticipated every need. She was bewildered, faint from want of food, and everything seemed unreal.

For the moment she could just sit still and be waited on by the soft-footed, soft-spoken manservant of an Arab Chief.

"*Monseigneur* begs that you will excuse him until this evening. He will return in time for dinner," he murmured as he handed her a *cous-cous*.

Diana looked up blankly.

"*Monseigneur?*"

"My master. The Sheik."

She flushed scarlet and her face hardened. Suffering in any form was new to her, and her hatred of the man who had made her suffer grew with every breath she drew.

The Frenchman came back with coffee.

"*Monseigneur* dines at eight. At what hour will *Madame* have tea?" he asked as he cleared away and folded up the table.

Diana choked back the sarcastic retort that sprang to her lips.

She gave an answer indifferently and turned her back on him. When she looked again he was gone, and she heaved a sigh of relief.

The night before she had taken in nothing of her surroundings, her eyes had been held only by the man who had dominated everything.

Here, also, were the same luxurious appointments as in the sleeping-room. She appreciated that the rugs and hangings were exquisite, the former were Persian and the latter of a thick black material, heavily embroidered in silver.

The main feature of the room was a big black divan heaped with huge cushions covered with dull black silk.

At one end of the tent was a small bookcase, and at the other end, near the open doorway, a little portable writing-table.

She crossed the tent to the little bookcase and knelt beside it curiously. What did a Francophile-Arab read? Novels, probably, that would harmonise with the atmosphere that she dimly sensed in her surroundings.

But it was not novels that filled the bookcase. There were books of sport and travel, with several volumes on veterinary surgery. They were all in French, and had all been frequently handled; many of them had pencilled notes in the margins written in Arabic.

One shelf was filled entirely with the works of one man, a certain *Vicomte* Raoul de Saint Hubert. With the exception of one novel, which Diana only glanced at hastily, they were all books of travel.

From the few scribbled words in the front of each, Diana could see that they had all been sent to the Arab by the author himself—one even was dedicated to "My friend, Ahmed Ben Hassan, Sheik of the Desert."

She put the books back with a puzzled frown. It was an unexpected glimpse into the personality of the Arab who had captured her, and he seemed to become infinitely more sinister.

She looked at her watch with sudden apprehension. The day was wearing away quickly. Soon he would come. Her breath came quick and short and the tears welled up in her eyes.

"I mustn't! I mustn't!" she whispered in a kind of desperation. "If I cry again I shall go mad."

She forced them back, and crossing to the big black divan that she had scorned before she dropped down among the soft cushions. She was so tired, and her head throbbed persistently.

She was asleep when the servant brought tea, but she started up as he put the tray on a stool be-her.

"It is *Madame*'s own tea. If she will be good enough to say if it is made to her taste," he said anxiously, as if his whole happiness were contained in the tiny teapot at which he was frowning deprecatingly.

His assiduity jarred Diana's newfound jangling nerves. She recognised that he was sincere in his efforts to please her, but just now they only seemed an added humiliation.

She longed to shout "Go away!" like an angry schoolboy, but she managed to give him the information he wanted.

The longing for fresh air and the desire to see what place she had been brought to grew irresistible as the evening came nearer. She went to the open doorway. A big awning stretched before it, supported on lances.

She stepped out from under its shade and looked about her wonderingly. It was a big oasis—bigger than any she had seen before. In front of the tent there was an open space with a thick belt of palm trees beyond.

The rest of the camp lay behind the Chief's tent. The place was alive with men and horses. There were some camels in the distance, but it was the horses that struck Diana principally. They were everywhere, some tethered, some wandering loose, some exercising in the hands of grooms.

Mounted Arabs on the outskirts of the oasis crossed her view occasionally. There were groups of men engaged on various duties all round her.

She turned at a sudden noise near her. A biting, screaming chestnut fury was coming past close to the tent, taking complete charge of the two men who clung, yelling, to his head.

He was stripped, but Diana recognised him at once. The one brief view she had had of his small, vicious head as he shot past her elbow the evening before was written on her brain for all time.

He came to a halt opposite Diana, refusing to move, his ears laid close to his head, quivering all over, snatching continually at his grooms, who seemed unable to cope with him.

The French servant, coming from behind the tent, spoke to Diana with his pleasant smile.

"He is rightly named Shaitan, *Madame,* for he is assuredly possessed of a devil," he said.

The chestnut at that moment, with a violent plunge, broke away from the men who were holding him and headed for the edge of the oasis with the Arabs streaming after him.

"The mounted men will catch him," he added

with a little laugh, in response to Diana's exclamation.

"Is he amusing himself, or is it really vice?" she asked.

"Pure vice, *Madame*. He has killed three men."

Diana looked at him incredulously, for his tone was casual and his manner did not indicate any undue feeling.

"He ought to be shot," she said indignantly.

The man shrugged.

"Monseigneur is fond of him."

And so because *Monseigneur* was fond of him the vicious animal was surrounded with every care that his master's pleasure might not be interfered with. Evidently the lives of his wretched people were of less value to him than that of a favourite horse!

"The horses are magnificent," Diana said, "but they are bigger than any Arabians I have seen before."

"They are a special breed, *Madame*," replied the Frenchman. "The tribe has been famous for them for generations. *Monseigneur*'s horses are known through all the Barbary States, and as far as France."

Diana looked at him speculatively.

There was an inflection in his voice each time he mentioned his master that indicated a devotion that she was unable to accredit to the brute from whose treatment she was still suffering. But her thoughts were broken into abruptly.

"There is *Monseigneur*," the servant exclaimed.

He spoke as if she, too, must be glad of his coming.

Did the valet imagine for one moment that she was there of her own free will? Or was it all a part of the hypocrisy in which she seemed to be enveloped? She flashed one glance at the horsemen riding through the belt of trees that fringed the oasis and an icy perspiration chilled her from head to foot.

She shrank back under the awning and into the coolness of the tent, raging against the mastering fear that she could not overcome. But just inside the open doorway she stood firm; even her fear could make her go no further.

She would meet him here, not cowering in the inner room like a trembling creature skulking in the furthest corner of its cage. That much pride at least was left.

From the shelter of the tent she watched the troop arrive at the open space before her.

The horse the Sheik was riding was jet black, and Diana looked from the beautiful creature's satiny coat to the man's white robes with angry contempt.

"Black and white! Black and white! *Mountebank!*" she muttered through her clenched teeth.

Then as he swung to the ground every thought fell from her but the terror he inspired. She waited, breathless, the swift racing of her heart an actual physical pain.

He lingered, fondling the great black horse,

and even after it had been led away he stood looking after it, talking to a tall young Arab who had ridden in with him. At last he turned and came leisurely towards the tent.

He paused at the door to speak to the Frenchman, a picturesque, barbaric figure, the profile of his lean face clean cut against the evening sky.

Then he swept into the tent, and she drew back from him with lowered eyes. She would not look at him; she would not meet his look. His presence was an offence, and she was scorched with shame.

Her breast heaved stormily with the rapid beating of her heart, but she held herself proudly erect. He crossed the tent with a long noiseless stride.

"I hope that Gaston took care of you properly and gave you everything that you wanted?" he asked easily.

"Is it not time that this ended? Haven't you done enough?" she burst out passionately. "Why have you committed this outrage?"

There was no answer, and she grew utterly reckless.

"Do you think that you can keep me here, you fool? That I can vanish into the desert and no notice will be taken of my disappearance—that no enquiries will be made?"

"There will be no enquiries," he answered calmly.

She ground the heel of her boot into the soft carpet.

"There *will* be enquiries," she choked furiously.

"I am not such a nonentity that nothing will be done when I am missed. The English authorities will make the French Government find out who is responsible, and you will have to pay for what you have done."

He laughed—the little amused laugh that sent the same cold feeling of dread through her that she had felt the day before.

"The French Government has no jurisdiction over me. I am not subject to it. I am an independent Chief, my own master. I recognise no government. My tribe obey me and only me."

"When I am missed . . ." she began desperately, trying to keep a bold front, but her assurance was leaving her.

"You will not be missed for so long that it will be too late," he replied drily.

"Too late! What do you mean?" she gasped.

"Your own plans will stop any possibility of enquiry for some time to come."

She put her hands to her head to try to stop the throbbing in her temples.

"You engaged a caravan in the charge of Mustafa Ali," he went on evenly, "to travel in the desert for a month. You set out from Biskra, but your intention was at the end of the time to travel northward to Oran and there dismiss the caravan.

"From there you were to cross to Marseilles, then to Cherbourg, where you would embark for America to follow your brother, who has already started."

She listened breathlessly with an ever-increasing fear growing in her eyes. The slow, casual voice detailing her itinerary with the quiet certainty of perfect knowledge filled her with a terror that made her want to scream.

"How do you know—all—this?" she whispered with dry lips that trembled.

"I wished to know. It was quite simple."

Her anger flamed up again.

"Is it money that you want? Are you holding me for ransom?"

But her scornful voice faltered and died away on the last word, and it did not need his silence to convince her that it was no question of ransom.

She wrung her hands convulsively and a great shudder shook her. Then in her despair a faint ray of hope came.

"Mustafa Ali, or one of the caravan men, may have given the alarm already in Biskra—if you have not—murdered them all," she whispered jerkily.

"I have not murdered them all," he rejoined shortly, "but Mustafa Ali will not give any alarm in Biskra."

"Why?"

She tried to keep silent, but the question was forced from her, and she waited tensely for his answer.

"There was no need for any murder," he continued sarcastically. "When you come to know me better you will realise that I do not leave too much to chance.

"It was very simple. *Voyons!* You paid

Mustafa Ali well to guide you in the desert. I paid him better to lead you to me. I paid him well enough to make him content to remove himself from Biskra, to where he is unknown, and where he can build up for himself a new reputation as a caravan leader."

There was another silence and Diana's hands went gropingly to her throat. It had been no chance affair then—no accidental meeting that the Arab Chief had turned to his own account, but an organised outrage that had been carefully planned from the beginning.

From the very outset she had been a dupe. She ground her teeth with rage. Her suave, subservient guide had been leading her the whole time towards the man who had bought him to betray her trust.

Mustafa Ali's shifting eyes, his desire to hurry her from the oasis where they had rested at midday, and his tone were all explained. He had acted well.

The last touch—the imaginary wound that had toppled him slowly out of his saddle—had been a masterpiece, she reflected bitterly.

Nothing had been omitted to make the outrage a success. The horse that had been given to her to ride was the Sheik's, trained to his whistle. Even her revolver had been tampered with. She had not missed, as she had thought.

She remembered the noise, the fleeting vision she had had in the hotel at Biskra. It had been someone in her room, Mustafa Ali himself, or one of his men, who had stolen in and substituted the blank cartridges.

The net that she had felt closing round her earlier in the afternoon seemed wrapped round her now inextricably, drawing tighter and tighter, smothering her. She gasped for breath.

The sinking sun seemed suddenly to leap up wildly into the heavens; then she pulled herself together with a tremendous effort.

"Why have you done this?" she murmured faintly.

Then for a moment her heart stood still, her eyes dilating.

He had come close behind her, and she waited in an agony, until he caught her to him, crushing her against him, forcing her head back on his arm.

"Because one day in Biskra, four weeks ago, I saw you and I wanted you. What I want I take. You played into my hands. You arranged a tour in the desert. The rest was easy."

Her eyes were shut, the long dark lashes quivering on her pale cheeks so that she could not see his face, but she felt him draw her closer to him and then his fierce kisses on her mouth.

She struggled frantically, but she was helpless, and he laughed softly as he kissed her lips, her hair, and her eyes passionately.

He stood quite still, but she felt the heavy beating of his heart under her cheek, and understood dimly the passion that she had aroused in him.

She had experienced his tremendous strength. She knew that her life was in his hands, that he could break her with his lean brown fingers like a toy is broken, and all at once she felt pitifully weak and frightened.

She was utterly in his power and at his mercy —the mercy of an Arab who was merciless.

She gave in suddenly, and lay quietly in his arms.

She had touched the lowest depths of degradation; he could do nothing more to her than he had done.

For the moment she could fight no further, she was worn out and utterly weary. She had suffered so much that nothing more mattered.

The strong arms round her tightened slowly.

"Look at me," he said in the soft slow voice that seemed habitual to him, and which contrasted oddly with the neat, clipping French that he spoke.

She shivered and her dark lashes flickered for a moment.

"Look at me."

His voice was just as slow, just as soft, but into it had crept an inflection that was unmistakable.

Twenty-four hours ago Diana Mayo had not known the meaning of the word *fear*, and had never in all her life obeyed anyone against her inclination, but in twenty-four hours she had lived through years of emotions.

For the first time she had pitted her will against a will that was stronger than her own, for the first time she had met an arrogance that was greater and a determination that was firmer than hers.

For the first time she had met a man who had failed to bow to her wishes, whom a look had been powerless to transform into a willing slave.

In the few hours that had elapsed she had learned fear, a terrible fear that left her sick with apprehension, and she was learning obedience.

Obedient now, she forced herself to lift her eyes to his, and the shamed blood surged slowly into her cheeks. His dark, passionate eyes burnt into her like a hot flame. His encircling arms were like bands of fire, scorching her. His touch was torture.

Helpless, like a trapped wild thing, she lay against him, panting, trembling, her wide eyes fixed on him, held against their will.

He smiled down at her suddenly.

"Bon Dieu! Do you know how beautiful you are?"

The sound of his voice seemed to break a spell that had kept her dumb. She struggled again to free herself.

"Let me go!" she cried piteously.

It was her complete immunity to him that she prayed for, but he chose wilfully to misunderstand her. The passion faded from his eyes, giving place to a gleam of mockery.

"There is plenty of time. Gaston is the most discreet servant. We shall hear him when he comes," he said with a low laugh.

But she persisted with the courage of desperation.

"When will you let me go?"

With an exclamation of impatience he put her from him roughly, and going to the divan flung himself down on the cushions, lit a cigarette, and picked up a magazine that was lying on an inlaid stool beside him.

She bit her lips to keep back the hysterical sobs that rose in her throat, nerving herself with clenched hands, and followed him.

"You *must* tell me. I *must* know. When will you let me go?"

He turned a page with deliberation, and flicked the ash from his cigarette before looking up.

A heavy scowl gathered on his face, and his eyes swept her from head to foot with a slow scrutiny that made her shrink.

"When I am tired of you," he said coldly.

She shuddered violently and turned away with a little moan, stumbling blindly towards the inner room, but as she reached the curtains his voice arrested her.

He had thrown aside the magazine and was lying back on the divan, his long limbs stretched out indolently, his hands clasped behind his head.

"You make a very charming boy," he said lightly, with a faint smile, "but it was not a boy that I saw in Biskra. You understand?"

Beyond the curtains she stood for a moment, shaking all over, her face hidden in her hands, able to relax a little the hold that she was keeping on herself.

Yes! She understood plainly enough. The understanding had already been forced upon her.

It was an order from one who was prepared to compel his commands, to make herself more attractive with all that it implied in the eyes of the man who held her in his power.

A man who looked at her as no other man had ever dared to look, with appraising criticism that made her acutely conscious of her sex, that made her feel like a slave exposed for sale in a public market.

She must take off the boyish clothes that somehow seemed to lend her courage, and substitute to gratify the whim of the savage in the next room. She must wear a dress that revealed more intimately the slender lines of her figure and intensified her beauty.

She went to the dressing-table with lagging feet, and stared resentfully at the white face and haggard eyes that looked back at her from the mirror. It was like the face of a stranger.

Tonight she did not dress to please herself. Her face was set, her eyes almost black with rage, but behind the rage there was lurking apprehension.

She started at every sound that came from the adjoining room. Her fingers, wet with perspiration, seemed almost unable to fulfil their task.

She hated him, she hated herself, she hated

her beauty, which had brought this horror upon her. She would have rebelled if she had dared, but instinctively she hurried—fear had already driven her so far.

But when she was ready she did not move from the table beside which she stood. Fear had forced her to haste, but her still-struggling pride would not permit her to obey her fear any further.

She raised her eyes to the glass again, glowering angrily at the pale reflection, and the old obstinacy mingled with the new pain that filled them.

The wave of anger that went through her rushed the colour into her face and she leaned nearer the glass with a little murmur of satisfaction that stopped abruptly as her fingers gripped the edge of the table.

Then she continued staring into the mirror not at her own face but at the white robes that appeared behind her head, blotting out the limited view she had had of the room.

The Sheik was standing behind her.

He had come with the peculiar noiseless tread that she had noticed before.

He swung her round to look at her and she writhed under his eyes of admiration, straining from him as far as his grip allowed.

Holding her with one hand, he took her chin in the other and tilted her face up to his with a little smile.

"Don't look so frightened. I don't want anything more deadly than some soap and water. Surely even an Arab may be allowed to wash his hands?"

His mocking voice and his taunt of fear stung her, but she would not answer, and with a laugh and a shrug he let her go, picking up a razor from the table and lounging into the bathroom.

With crimson cheeks Diana fled into the outer room. His manner could not have been more casual if she had been his wife for a dozen years.

She waited for him in a tumult of emotions, but with the advent of Gaston and dinner, he returned to the attitude of dispassionate, courteous host that he had assumed when he first came in.

He was a few minutes late, and apologised gravely as he sat down opposite to her. He maintained the attitude throughout dinner, and conscious of the watching manservant Diana made herself reply to his easy conversation.

He talked mainly of the desert and the sport that it offered, as if he had studied her tastes and chosen the topic to please her.

And all the time she was aware acutely of his constant surveillance. Reluctantly her own furtive glance was drawn frequently to his face, and always his dark fierce eyes were watching her with a steadiness that racked her nerves.

The dinner seemed interminable, and yet she wished that it would never end. While the servant was in the room she was safe; the thought of his going sent a cold shudder through her.

With the coffee came a huge Persian hound,

almost upsetting the Frenchman in the entrance in his frantic endeavour to precede him through the doorway. He flung his long grey body across the Sheik's knees with a whine of pleasure and then turned his head to growl at Diana.

But the growl died away quickly, and he lumbered down and came to her side curiously, eyeing her for a moment and then thrusting his big head against her.

The Sheik laughed.

"You are honoured. Kopec makes few friends."

She did not answer. The natural reply was almost certain to provoke a retort that she did not desire, so she remained silent, smoothing the hound's rough coat.

For some minutes the Sheik sat silent, then he got up, and followed by the hound he left the tent.

Diana retired onto the thick rug beside the bookcase. For a moment she was alone, free of the watching eyes that seemed to be burning into her.

She dropped her head on her knees with a little whimper of weariness. She was tired in mind and body, exhausted with the emotions that had shaken her until she knew that no matter what happened in the future the Diana of yesterday was dead.

Her tired body shrank from the struggle that must recommence so soon. If he would only spare her until this numbing weariness that made her so powerless should lessen.

She heard his voice at the door. The thick rugs deadened the sound of his movements, but she knew instinctively that he had come in and gone to the divan.

"Come here—Diana."

She started, for a moment hardly recognising the Gallic rendering of her name, and then flushed angrily without answering or moving.

It was a very little thing to stir her after all that he had done, but the use of her name flamed the anger that had been almost swamped in fear.

She sat with her hands gripped tightly in her lap, breathing rapidly, her eyes dark with apprehension.

"Come here," he repeated sharply.

Still she took no notice, but the face that he could not see was growing very white.

"I am not accustomed to having my orders disobeyed," he said at last, very slowly.

"And I am not accustomed to obeying orders," she retorted fiercely, though her lips were trembling.

"You will learn." The sinister accent of his voice almost shattered her remaining courage.

With a choking cry she leapt to her feet suddenly and fled from him, back till the side of the tent stopped her and she stood, with wide-flung arms, gripping the black and silver hangings until he reached her.

Stooping, he disengaged her clinging fingers from the heavy drapery and drew her hands slowly together up to his breast with a little smile.

"Come," he whispered, his passionate eyes devouring her.

She fought against the fascination with which they dominated her, resisting him dumbly with tight-locked lips till he held her palpitating in his arms.

"Little fool," he said with a deepening smile. "Better me than my men."

The gibe broke her silence.

"Oh, you brute! You brute!" she wailed, until his kisses silenced her.

Chapter
Four

"A month! Thirty-one days! Oh, God! Only thirty-one days. It seems a lifetime. Only a month since I left Biskra. A month! A month!"

Diana flung herself onto her face, burying her head deeply into the cushions of the divan.

She did not cry. The complete breakdown of the first night had never been repeated. Tears of shame and anger had risen in her eyes often, but she would not let them fall. She would not give her captor the satisfaction of knowing that he could make her weep.

Her pride was dying hard. Her mind travelled back slowly over the days and nights of anguished revolt, the perpetual clash of will against will, the enforced obedience that had made up this month of horror.

A month of experience of such bitterness that she wondered dully how she still had the courage to rebel. For the first time in her life she had had to obey. For the first time in her life she was of no account.

For the first time she had been made conscious of the inferiority of her sex.

He was an Arab, to whom the feelings of a woman were nonexistent. He had taken her to please himself and he kept her to please himself, to amuse him in his moments of relaxation.

But she had not been prepared for the ceaseless activity of the man whose prisoner she was. His life was hard, strenuous, and occupied.

His days were full, partly with the magnificent horses that he bred, and partly with tribal affairs that took him from the camp for hours at a time.

Upon one or two occasions he had been away for the whole night and had come back at daybreak with all the evidences of hard riding.

Some days she rode with him, but when he

had not the time or the inclination, the French valet went with her.

A beautiful grey thoroughbred called Silver Star was kept for her use, and sometimes on his back she was able to forget for a little time.

So the moments of relaxation were less frequent than they might have been, and it was only in the evenings when Gaston had come and gone for the last time and she was alone with the Sheik that an icy hand seemed to close down over her heart.

And, according to his mood, he noticed or ignored her. He demanded implicit obedience to his lightest whim with the unconscious tyranny of one who has always been accustomed to command.

He ruled his unruly followers despotically, and it was obvious that while they loved him they feared him equally. She had even seen Yusef, his lieutenant, cringe from the heavy scowl that she had, herself, learned to dread.

"You treat them like dogs," she said to him once. "Are you not afraid that one day they will rise against you and murder you?"

And he had only shrugged his shoulders and laughed, the same low laugh of amusement that never failed to make her shiver.

The only person whose devotion seemed untinged by any conflicting sentiment was the French valet, Gaston.

It was the Sheik's complete indifference to anything beyond his own will that stung her most.

He treated her supplications and invectives with a like unconcern. The paroxysms of wild rage that filled her periodically made no impression on him.

But in the grasp of his lean, brown fingers and under the stare of his dark, fierce eyes her own would drop, and the frantic words would die from her lips.

She was physically afraid of him, and she hated him and loathed herself for the fear he inspired. And her fear was legitimate. His strength was abnormal, and behind it was the lawlessness and absolution that allowed free rein to his savage impulses. He held life and death in his hand.

A few days after he had taken her she had seen him chastise a servant.

She did not know what the man's fault had been, but the punishment seemed out of all proportion to anything that could be imagined.

She had watched, fascinated with horror, until he had tossed away the murderous whip, and without a second glance at the limp, blood-stained heap that huddled on the ground with suggestive stillness had strolled back unconcerned to the tent.

The sight had sickened her and haunted her perpetually. His callousness horrified her even more than his cruelty. She hated him with all the strength of her proud, passionate nature.

Even his personal beauty was an additional cause of offence. She hated him the more for his handsome face and graceful, muscular body.

His only redeeming virtue in her eyes was his

total lack of vanity, which she grudgingly admitted. He was as unconscious of himself as was the wild animal with which she compared him.

"He is like a tiger," she murmured deep into the cushions, with a shiver, "a graceful, cruel, merciless beast."

A hand on her shoulder made her start up with a cry. Usually her nerves were in better control, but the thick rugs deadened every sound, and she had not expected him so soon.

He had been out since dawn and had come in much past his usual time, and had been having a belated siesta in the adjoining room.

Angry with herself, she bit her lip and pushed the tumbled hair off her forehead.

He dropped onto the divan beside her and lit the inevitable cigarette; he smoked continuously every moment that he was not in the saddle.

She glanced at him covertly. He was lying with his head thrown back against the cushions, idly blowing smoke-rings and watching them drift towards the open doorway.

"Zilah is careless. Insist that she put away your boots and does not leave your clothes lying on the floor. There was a scorpion in the bathroom today," he said lazily, stretching out his long legs.

She flushed hotly, as she always did when he made any casual reference to the intimacy of their life. She felt the warm blood pouring over her face now, up to the roots of her bright hair.

She gave a sigh of relief when Gaston came in bringing a little tray with two filigree-cased cups of coffee.

"I have brought coffee; *Madame*'s tea is finished," he murmured in tones of deepest distress, and with a gesture that conveyed a national calamity.

There had been just enough tea taken on the tour to last a month. It was another pin-prick, another reminder. She set her teeth, moving her head angrily, and found herself looking into a pair of mocking eyes, and, as always, her own dropped.

A noise outside attracted her, and she wandered to the doorway and out under the awning.

The Sheik with Gaston and Yusef stood watching a mad, rampaging colt that was being held with difficulty by two or three men, who clung to him tenaciously in spite of his efforts to break away.

The frantic colt was going to be broken. It was already saddled. Several additional men ran forward, and between them the horse was forcibly held for a moment—only for a moment, but it was long enough for the man who leapt like a flash onto his back.

Amazed for the moment at the sudden unaccustomed weight, the colt paused, and then reared straight up, till it seemed to Diana that he must fall backward and crush the man who was clinging to him.

The end came quickly. With a twisting heave of his whole body he shot the Arab over his head, who landed with a dull thud, while the men who had been holding the colt dashed in and secured him before he was aware of his liberty.

Laughing, the man came to the Sheik with a shrug of the shoulders and outspread eloquent hands.

They spoke together for a moment, too low for Diana to hear, and then Ahmed Ben Hassan went alone into the middle of the ring.

Diana's breath came more quickly. She guessed his intention before he reached the colt.

"*Monseigneur* will try?" she asked Gaston, who was standing watching.

"Yes, *Madame*, he will try."

The empty saddle was filled, and a curious hush came over the watching crowd. Diana looked on with bright, hard eyes, her heart beating heavily. She longed passionately that the colt might kill him, and, at the same time, illogically, she wanted to see him master the infuriated animal.

The sporting instinct in her acknowledged and responded to the fight that was going on before her eyes. She hated him and she hoped that he might die, but she was forced to admire the wonderful horsemanship that she was watching.

The Sheik sat like a rock, and every effort made to unseat him was unsuccessful. The colt plunged wildly, making furious blind dashes backwards and forwards, stopping dead in the hope of dislodging his rider, twirling round suddenly until it seemed impossible that he could keep his feet.

Then he started rearing, straight up, his forelegs beating the air, higher and higher, and then down, to commence again without a moment's breathing-space.

Diana heard Gaston's breath whistle through his teeth.

"Look, *Madame!*" he cried sharply, and Diana saw the Sheik give a quick glance behind him, and, as the colt shot up again, almost perpendicular, with a jerk he pulled him deliberately over backwards, leaping clear with a tremendous effort as the horse crushed to the ground.

He was in the saddle again almost before the dazed creature had struggled to his feet. And then began a scene that Diana never forgot.

It was the final struggle that was to end in defeat for either man or horse, a hideous exhibition of brute strength and merciless cruelty.

Diana was almost sick with horror from the beginning; she longed to turn away, but her eyes clung fascinated to the battle that was going on.

She was shaking all over and her hands were clenching and unclenching as she stared at the man, who seemed a part of the horse he was sitting so closely.

Would it never end? She did not care now which killed the other, she cared only that it would stop. The man's endurance seemed mere bravado. She clutched Gaston's arm with a hand that was wringing wet.

"It is horrible," she gasped with an accent of loathing.

"It is necessary," he replied quietly.

"Nothing can justify that," she cried passionately.

"Your pardon, *Madame*. He must learn. He killed a man this morning, threw him, and what you call in English 'savaged' him."

Diana hid her face in her hands.

"I can't bear it," she said pitifully.

A few minutes later Gaston clicked his tongue against his teeth.

"See, *Madame*. It is over," he said gently.

She looked up fearfully. The Sheik was standing on the ground beside the colt, who was swaying slowly from side to side with heaving sides and head held low to the earth, dripping blood and foam. And as she looked he tottered and collapsed, exhausted.

Diana turned away with an exclamation of disgust, and she went slowly back into the tent, shaken with what she had seen. She closed her eyes in a sudden agony, and then stiffened at the sound of his voice outside.

He came in laughing, a cigarette dangling from one blood-stained hand, while with the other he wiped the perspiration from his forehead, leaving a dull red smear.

She shrank from him, looking at him with blazing eyes.

"You are a brute, a beast, a devil! I hate you!" she choked furiously.

For a moment an ugly look crossed his face, and then he laughed again.

"Hate me, by all means, *ma belle,* but let your hatred be thorough. I detest mediocrity," he said lightly, as he passed on into the other room.

When he came back he was immaculate and well-groomed, and he was very different from the dishevelled, blood-stained savage of half an hour before. She shot a nervous glance at him, remembering her outburst, but he was not angry.

He did not speak for a long time, but sat on the divan, apparently absorbed in his thoughts.

Yet when he called her, with a swift revulsion of feeling she wished he had kept silent. She went to him slowly, too unnerved tonight to struggle against him.

He pulled her down on the divan beside him, and before she realised what he was doing he slipped a long jade necklace over her head.

For a moment she looked stupidly at the wonderful thing, almost unique in the purity of its colour and the marvellous carving on the uniform square pieces of which it was composed, and then with a low cry she tore it off and flung it on the ground.

"How dare you?" she gasped.

"You don't like it?" he asked in his low, unruffled voice, his eyebrows raised in real or assumed surprise. "Yet it matches your dress."

Lightly his long fingers touched the folds of green silk swathed across the youthful curve of her breast.

He glanced at an open box filled with shimmering stones on a low stool beside him.

"Pearls are too cold and diamonds too banal for you," he said slowly. "You should wear nothing but jade. It is the colour of the evening sky against the sunset of your hair."

He had never spoken like that to her before, or used that tone of voice. His methods had been more fierce than tender.

She glanced up swiftly at his face, but it baffled her. There was no love in his eyes or even desire, nothing but an unusual gentleness.

"Perhaps you would prefer the diamonds and the pearls," he went on, pointing disdainfully at the box.

"No, no. I hate them! I hate them all! I will not wear your jewels. You have no right to think that I am that kind of woman," she cried hysterically.

"You do not like them? *Bon Dieu!* None of the other women ever refused them. On the contrary, they never could get enough," he said with a laugh.

Diana looked up with a startled glance, a look of horror dawning in her eyes.

"Other women?" she repeated blankly.

"You didn't suppose you were the first, did you?" he asked with brutal candour. "Don't look at me like that. They were not like you, they came to me willingly enough—too willingly. Allah! How they bored me! I tired of them before they tired of me."

She flung her arm across her eyes with a dry sob, straining away from him. She had never thought of that. In the purity of her mind it had never occurred to her.

She was only one of many, one of a succession of mistresses, taken and discarded at his whim. She writhed with the shame that filled her.

"Oh, you hurt me!" she whispered very low.

Then anger killed all other feeling. He had loosened his arm about her, and she wrenched herself free and sprang to her feet.

"I hate you, do you understand? I hate you! I hate you!"

He lit a cigarette leisurely and moved into a more comfortable position on the divan before answering.

"So you have already told me this afternoon," he said at length coolly, "and with reiteration your remark becomes less convincing, *ma chère*."

Her anger ebbed away. She was too tired to be angry. She was humiliated and hurt, and the man before her had it in his power to hurt her more, but she was at his mercy and tonight she could not fight.

She pushed the hair off her forehead with a heavy sigh and looked at the Sheik's long length stretched out on the couch, the steely strength of his limbs patent even in the indolent attitude in which he was lying.

His brown handsome face was inscrutable as it always was, and the feeling of helplessness came back with renewed force and with it the sense of her own pitiful weakness.

"Have you never felt pity for a thing that was weaker than yourself? Have you never spared anything or anyone in all your life? Have you nothing in your nature but cruelty? Are all Arabs like you?" she asked shakily. "Has love never even made you merciful?"

He glanced up at her with a harsh laugh, and shook his head.

"Love? *Connais pas!* Yes, I do," he added with swift mockery, "I love my horses."

"When you don't kill them."

"I am corrected. When I don't kill them."

There was something in his voice that made her reckless, that made her want to hurt him.

"If you give no love to the—the women whom you bring here, do you give no love to the women of your harem? You have a harem, I suppose, somewhere?"

She braved him, but as she spoke she knew that she had only hurt herself and her voice faltered.

His hand reached out suddenly and he dragged her down into his arms again with a laugh.

"And if I have, are you jealous? What if the nights I spent away from you were passed in my harem—what then?"

"Then may Allah put it into the heart of one of your wives to poison you so that you never come back," she said fiercely.

"Allah! So beautiful and so bloodthirsty," he said in bantering reproof.

He turned her face up to his, smiling into her angry eyes with amusement.

"I have no harem and, thanks be to Allah, no wives, *chérie*. Does that please you?"

"Why should I care? It is nothing to me," she replied sharply, with a vivid blush.

He held her closer, looking deeply into her eyes, holding them as he could when he liked, in spite of her efforts to turn them away—a mesmerism she could not resist.

"Shall I make you care? Shall I make you love me? I can make women love me when I choose."

She went very white and her eyes flickered. She knew that he was only amusing himself, that he was utterly indifferent to her feelings, but it was a new form of torture that was more detestable than anything that had gone before it.

It infuriated her that he could even suggest that she could come to care for him, that she could ever look on him as anything but a brutal savage.

That he should class her with the other women he spoke of revolted her; she felt degraded, soiled as she had never felt before, and she had thought that she had felt the utmost humiliation of her position.

The colour rushed back into her face.

"I would rather you killed me," she cried passionately.

"So would I," he said drily, "for if you loved

me you would bore me and I should have to let you go. While as it is"—he laughed softly—"as it is I do not yet regret the chance that took me into Biskra that day."

He let her go and got up with a yawn, watching her approvingly as she crossed the tent.

The easy swing of her boyish figure and the defiant carriage of her head reminded him of one of his own thoroughbred horses.

She was as beautiful and as wild as they were.

And as he broke them so would he break her. She was nearly tamed now, but not quite, and, by Allah! it should be quite!

As he turned, his foot struck against the jade necklace lying on the rug where she had thrown it.

He picked it up and called her back. She came reluctantly, slowly, with mutinous eyes.

He held out the necklace silently, and silently she stared not at it but at him.

Her heart began to beat faster, and the colour slowly left her face.

"Take it. I wish it," he said quietly.

"No."

It was little more than a gasp.

"You will wear it to please me," he went on in the same soft voice, and the old hateful mockery crept into his eyes, "to please my artistic soul. I have an artistic soul even though I am only an Arab."

"I will not!"

The mockery was wiped out of his eyes in a flash, giving place to the usual ferocity, and his forehead knitted in the dreaded heavy scowl.

"Diana, obey me!"

She clenched her teeth on her lower lip until a rim of blood stained their whiteness.

If he would only shout or bluster like the average angry man, she felt that she could brave him longer, but the cold quiet rage that characterised him always was infinitely more sinister, and paralysed her with its silent force.

She had never heard him raise his voice in anger or quicken his usual slow, soft tone, but there was an inflection that came into his voice and a look that came into his eyes that was more terrible than any outburst.

She had seen his men shrink. She had seen a look from him silence a clamorous quarrel that had broken out among his followers too close to his own tent.

And that inflection was in his voice and that look was in his eyes now. It was no use to resist.

The fear of him was an agony. She would have to obey, as in the end he always forced her to obey.

She wrenched her eyes away from his compelling stare, her breasts heaving under the soft silk, her chin quivering, and reaching out blindly she took it from him.

The sudden chill of it against her bare breast

seemed to revive her courage that was not yet dead. She flung up her head, the transient colour flaming into her cheeks, but he drew her to him swiftly, and laid his hand over her mouth.

"I know, I know," he said coldly. "I am a brute and a beast and a devil. You need not tell me again. It commences to grow tedious."

His hand slipped to her shoulder, his fingers gripping the delicate, rounded arm.

"How much longer are you going to fight? Would it not be wiser after what you have seen today to recognise that I am master?"

"You mean that you will treat me as you treated the colt this afternoon?"

"I mean that you must realise that my will is law."

"And if I do not?"

He guessed rather than heard the words.

"Then I will teach you, and I think that you will learn—soon."

She quivered in his hands. It was a threat, but how much of it he meant to be taken literally she did not know. Again every ghastly detail of the afternoon passed with lightning speed through her mind. When he punished he punished mercilessly.

He was an Arab, and as a woman she need expect no mercy at his hands. His hands! She looked down for a second sideways at the fingers gripping her shoulder.

She knew already by bitter experience the

iron grip of his lean fingers and the compelling strength of his arms. Her quick imagination leapt ahead.

What she had already suffered would be nothing compared with what would be. The remembrance of the stained, huddled figure of the servant he had chastised rose before her.

As she battled with herself, still torn in her passionate desire to make her strong will and courageous spirit triumph over her cowardly woman's body that shrank instinctively from physical torture, his arm tightened round her.

She felt the hard muscles pressing against her shoulders and soft, bare neck, a suggestion of the force lying dormant beside her. She looked up at him slowly.

His expression was unchanged, his forehead was still drawn together in the heavy frown and there was no softening in his eyes. The cruel lines about his mouth were accentuated and the tiger-look in his face was more marked than ever.

He was not threatening idly; he meant what he said.

"You had better kill me," she said drearily.

"That would be to admit my own defeat," he replied coolly. "I do not kill a horse until I have proved beyond all possible doubt that I cannot tame it. With you I have no such proof. I can tame you and I will."

He paused. "But it is for you to choose and to choose tonight if you will obey me willingly or if I must make you. I have been very patient, but my patience is exhausted. Choose quickly."

Insensibly, he drew her closer to him till his arm felt like an inflexible steel hand about her, and with a shudder she thought of the coils of a great serpent closing round its victim.

She made a final effort to conquer herself, but a sudden nausea came over her, everything seemed to swim before her eyes, and she swayed against the man who was holding her.

Her bodily fear overruled her mind. She could not bear any more.

"I will obey you," she whispered heavily.

He took her chin in his fingers and jerked her head up sharply, staring at her intently until she felt that he was looking into her very soul.

"Good!" he said at length briefly. "You are wise."

He tilted her head further back, bending his own down until his lips were nearly touching hers. She shivered involuntarily, an anguished appeal leaping into her eyes.

He smiled ironically.

"Do you hate them so much, my kisses?"

She swallowed convulsively.

"You are at least candid if you are not complimentary."

He released her and turned away.

She reached the curtain that divided the two rooms, her heart beating wildly, giddy with the strain that she had gone through.

She paused a moment and looked back at him, amazed at her own temerity.

He had unbuttoned the flap of the tent and was standing in the entrance, looking out into the night.

Her eyes grew puzzled. Would she ever understand him?

Tonight he had given her a choice instead of simply enforcing his will; he had made her choose to save herself, he had proved his determination and his mastery over her.

And with his last words the unexpected gentleness had come into his voice again and the cruel lines about his mouth had relaxed in a smile of amusement.

It was the swift transition from ferocity to gentleness that she could never fathom.

She only knew that for some reason of his own he had spared her, and she feared him now more than ever.

Chapter
Five

Under the awning of the tent Diana was waiting for Gaston and the horses. She was wrought up up to the utmost pitch of excitement.

Ahmed Ben Hassan had been away since the previous day, and it was uncertain if he would return that night or the next. He had been vague as to how long he would be absent.

In the four weeks that had elapsed since she had promised him her obedience she had been very silent. Her fear and hatred of him grew daily.

She had learned to stifle the wild fits of rage and the angry words that leapt to her lips.

She had learned to obey—a reluctant obedience given with compressed lips and defiant eyes, but given, and with a silence that surprised even herself.

Lately he had left her very much alone; she had ridden with him almost daily until the last week, when he had announced curtly that in the meantime the length of her rides must be curtailed, and that Gaston would accompany her.

He had not offered any explanation, and she had not sought one.

She searched feverishly for means of flight, and now the Sheik's absence seemed to have given her the chance she had been waiting for.

In the solitude of the previous night she had tossed impatiently from side to side on the big couch, vainly trying to find some means of taking advantage of her comparative freedom to effect her escape.

Surely she could find some way of avoiding Gaston's vigilance? Excitement had kept her awake half the night, and in the morning she had had hard work to keep her agitation hidden and to appear as usual.

In her nervous terror she had even been

afraid to order the horses any earlier, lest the valet should suspect there was any reason behind the simple request.

After her *petit déjeuner* she had paced the tent, unable to sit still, dreading that any moment might bring the return of the Sheik and frustrate her hopes.

The horses were waiting, and Gaston was standing ready to hold her stirrup. She fondled the beautiful grey horse's soft nose and patted his satiny neck with a hand that trembled a little.

She loved the horse and today he should be the means of saving her. He responded to her caresses, gentling her with slobbering mouth and whinnying softly. With one last look at the big double tent and the rest of the camp behind it she mounted and rode away.

She had to exercise a rigid control over herself. She longed to put Silver Star into a hand gallop at once and shake off Gaston, but she was still too near the camp.

She must be patient and put a certain number of miles between herself and the possibility of pursuit before she attempted anything.

Too early an endeavour would only bring the whole horde in wild chase at her heels.

She took no heed of the time beyond the fact that it was passing quickly, and that if anything was to be done it must be done as soon as possible.

But Gaston, riding a few paces behind her, was very much alive to the hour and had looked several times at his watch. He ranged alongside of her now with a murmured apology.

"Pardon, *Madame*. It grows late."

She pulled up, and tilting her helmet back mopped her hot forehead, and, as she did so, a sharp breeze sprang up, the curious wind that comes and goes so rapidly in the desert. An idea flashed into her mind. It was a poor chance, but it might succeed. She shot a glance at Gaston.

He was looking in the opposite direction, and, raising her hand, she fluttered her handkerchief a moment in the breeze and then let it go. The wind carried it some distance away.

She gave a little cry and caught at the bridle of the valet's horse.

"Oh, Gaston, my handkerchief!" She pointed to where the morsel of cambric lay white against a rock.

With a comical exclamation of dismay he slipped to the ground and started to run across the sand.

She waited until he had got well on his way, sitting tense with shining eyes and thumping heart.

Then snatching off her helmet, she brought it down with a resounding smack on the hind-quarters of the servant's horse, stampeding it in the direction of the camp, and, wheeling Silver Star, headed for the north, deaf to Gaston's cries.

Wild with excitement and free to go at his own pace, her mount galloped swiftly and the wind whistled past Diana's ears.

To the possible fate of the little Frenchman

left on foot so far from the encampment she gave no heed.

For the moment she did not even think of him, she had no thought for anybody but herself.

Her ruse by its very simplicity had succeeded. She was free and she did not care about anything else. She had no plans or ideas of what she should do or where she should go beyond the fact that she would keep riding northward.

She had escaped from him and his cruelty; it was a nightmare that was over.

Silver Star had settled down into the steady tireless gallop for which Ahmed Ben Hassan's horses were famous. The little breeze had died away as quickly as it had sprung up, and it was very hot. Diana looked about her with glowing eyes.

For an hour or more the ground rose and fell in monotonous succession, and then quite suddenly she could see for miles.

About two miles away a few palm trees showed, clustering together, and she turned in their direction.

They probably meant a well, and it was time she rested her horse and herself. It was the tiniest little oasis, and she drew rein and dismounted with fears for the well she had hoped to find.

But there was one, very much silted up, and she set to work to clear it as well as she could to procure enough for herself and Silver Star, who was frantically trying to get to the water.

For the first time since she had shaken off

Gaston she began to think seriously. What she had done was madness. She had no food for herself or her horse, no water, and heaven alone knew where the next well might be.

Then the sudden panic to which she had given way subsided and her courage rose with a bound. It was only midday, and anything might happen between then and nightfall.

Of one thing only she was sure: she did not repent of what she had done. Behind her was Ahmed Ben Hassan and before her was possibly death, and death was preferable.

She lay down in the patch of shade with a resolute determination to banish from her mind the difficulties and dangers ahead of her. Time to think of them when they came.

For the next hour or two she must rest and escape the intense heat. She rolled over on her face with her head in her arms and tried to sleep, but she was too excited, and soon gave up the attempt.

And in any case, she argued with herself, she might sleep too long and lose precious time. She stretched luxuriously on the soft ground, thankful for the shade from the burning sun.

The past rose up, and rushed, uncontrolled, through her brain. Memories of moments when she had struggled against his caresses and he had mocked her helplessness with his great strength, when she had lain in his arms panting and exhausted, cold with fear and shrinking from his fierce kisses.

She had feared him as she had never believed it possible to fear. His face rose before her
clearly with all the expressions she had learned to
know and dread.

She tried to banish it, striving with all her
might to put him from her mind, twisting this way
and that, writhing on the soft sand as she struggled with the obsession that held her. She saw him
all the time plainly, as though he were there.

Would the recollection of the handsome
brown face haunt her forever with its fierce eyes
and cruel mouth?

She buried her head deeper in her arms, but
the vision persisted until with a scream she started
up with heaving chest and wild eyes, standing
rigid, staring towards the south with a desperate
fixedness that made her eyeballs ache.

The sense of his presence had been terribly
real.

She dropped onto the ground again with an
hysterical laugh, and pushed the thick hair off her
forehead wearily.

Silver Star laying his muzzle suddenly on her
shoulder made her start again violently with
heavy, beating heart.

"I'm nervous," she muttered, looking round
with a little shiver. "I shall go mad if I stay here
much longer."

The little oasis that she had hailed so joyfully
had become utterly repugnant and she was impatient to get away from it.

97

She climbed eagerly into the saddle, and, with rapid motion, she regained her calm and her spirits rose quickly.

She shook off the feeling of apprehension that had taken hold of her and her nervous fears died away. The afternoon was wearing away; already it was growing cooler.

Diana had seen no sign of human life since she had left Gaston hours before, and a little feeling of anxiety stirred faintly deep down in her heart.

She had got away from the level desert and was threading her way in and out of some low hills, which she felt were taking her out of her right course.

She was steering by the setting sun, which had turned the sky into a glory of golden crimson, but the intricate turnings amongst the rocky hills were bewildering. On rounding a particularly sharp turn, the rocks fell away suddenly and she rode out into open country.

Across the desert about a mile away she saw a party of Arabs coming towards her.

There were about fifty of them, the leader riding a big, black horse some little distance in front of his followers.

In the clear atmosphere they seemed nearer than they were.

They were a band of fighting men, for she could see their rifles clearly, and their close and orderly formation was anything but peaceful.

They filled her with the gravest misgivings. Only the worst might be expected from the wild, lawless tribesmen towards a woman alone amongst them.

She had fled from one hideousness to another which would be ten times more horrible!

The human beings she had prayed for were now a deadly menace, and she prayed as fervently that they might pass on and not notice her.

Perhaps it was not too late, perhaps they had not yet seen her and she might still slip away and hide in the twisting turnings of the defile.

She backed Silver Star farther into the shadow of the rock, but as she did so she saw that she had been seen.

The leader turned in his saddle and raised his hand high above his head, and with a wild shout and a great cloud of dust and sand his men checked their horses, dragging them back onto their haunches, while he galloped towards her alone.

And at the same moment an icy hand clutched at Diana's heart and a moan burst from her lips.

There was no mistaking him or the big black horse he rode.

For a moment she reeled with a sudden faintness, and then with a tremendous effort she pulled herself together.

Dragging her horse's head round, she urged him back along the track which she had just left, and behind her raced Ahmed Ben Hassan, spurring the great black stallion as he had never done before.

With a shy face and wild, hunted eyes Diana crouched forward on the grey's neck, saving him all she could and riding as she had never ridden in her life.

Utterly reckless, she urged the horse to his utmost pace, regardless of the rough, dangerous track. Perhaps she could still shake off her pursuer among the tortuous paths of the hills.

Better even an ugly toss and a broken neck than that he should take her again.

There was nothing now but the sheer speed of her horse to save her, and how long could she count on it?

Suddenly, a few minutes after she had left the hills behind, the Sheik's deep voice came clearly across the space between them.

"If you do not stop I will shoot your horse. I give you one minute."

She swayed a little in the saddle, clutching the grey's neck to steady herself, and for a moment she closed her eyes, but she did not falter for an instant.

She would not stop; nothing on earth should make her stop now.

But, because she knew the man, she kicked her feet clear of the stirrups.

He had said he would shoot and he would shoot, and if the grey shied or swerved a hair's breadth she would probably receive the bullet that was meant for him.

Better that! Yes, even better that!

Silver Star tore on headlong and the minute seemed a lifetime. Then even before she heard the report he bounded in the air and fell with a crash.

Diana was flung far forward and landed on some soft sand. For a moment she was stunned by the fall, then she staggered dizzily to her feet and stumbled back to the prostrate horse.

He was lashing out wildly with his heels, making desperate efforts to rise. And as she reached him the black horse dashed alongside, stopping suddenly and rearing straight up.

The Sheik leapt to the ground and ran towards her. He caught her wrist and flung her out of his way, and she lay where she had fallen, every nerve in her body quivering.

She was beaten and with the extinguishing of her last hope all her courage failed her. She gave way to sheer, overwhelming terror, utterly cowed.

Every faculty was suspended, swallowed up in the one dominating force, the dread of his voice and the dread of the touch of his hands.

She heard a second report and knew that he had put Silver Star out of his misery, and then, in a few seconds, his voice beside her. She got up unsteadily, shrinking from him.

"Why are you here, and where is Gaston?"

In a stifled voice she told him everything.

What did it matter? If she tried to be silent he would force her to speak.

He made no comment, and bringing his horse nearer tossed her up roughly into the saddle and swung up behind her, the black breaking at once into the usual headlong gallop.

Ahmed Ben Hassan did not go back through the defile, he turned into a little path which Diana had overlooked and which skirted the hills.

In about half an hour the troop met them, riding slowly from the opposite direction.

She did not raise her eyes as they approached, but she heard Yusef's clear tenor voice calling out to the Sheik, who answered shortly as the men fell in behind him.

She knew that it had been madness from the first. She should have known that it could never succeed, that she could never reach civilisation alone.

She had been a fool ever to imagine that she could win through.

The chance that had thrown her again into the Sheik's power might just as easily have thrown her into the hands of any other Arab.

Luck had helped Ahmed Ben Hassan even as she herself had unknowingly played into his hands when he had captured her first.

Fate was with him. It was useless to try and struggle against him anymore.

She lifted her head for the first time and looked at the magnificent sky.

The sun had almost set, going down in a ball

of molten fire. It was a country of marvellous beauty, and Diana's heart gave a sudden throb as she realised that she was going back to it all.

She was drooping wearily, unable to sit upright any longer, and once or twice she jolted heavily against the man who rode behind her.

His nearness had ceased to revolt her; she thought of it with a dull feeling of wonder.

She had even a sense of relief at the thought of the strength so close to her.

Her eyes rested on his hands, showing brown and muscular under the folds of his white robes. She knew the power of those long, lean fingers, which could, when he liked, be gentle enough.

Her eyes filled with sudden tears, but she blinked them back before they fell. She wanted desperately to cry.

A wave of terrible loneliness went over her, a feeling of desolation, and a strange, incomprehensible yearning for what she did not know.

She had drifted into oblivion when she was awakened by a jerk that threw her back violently against the Sheik, but she was too tired to more than barely understand that they had stopped for something, and that there were palm trees near her.

She felt herself lifted down and a cloak wrapped round her, and then she remembered nothing more.

* * *

She awoke slowly, shaking off a persistent drowsiness by degrees. She was still tired, but the desperate weariness was gone and she was conscious of a feeling of well-being and security.

In a few moments she was wide awake, and found that she was lying across the saddle in front of the Sheik, and that he was holding her in the crook of his arm. Her head was resting just over his heart, and she could feel the regular beat beneath her cheek.

Wrapped warmly and held securely by his strong arm, it was enough for the moment to lie with relaxed muscles, to have to make no effort of any kind, to feel the soothing rush of the wind against her face.

With a start she realised fully whose arm was round her, and whose breast her head was resting on.

Her heart beat with sudden violence. What was the matter with her?

Why did she not shrink from the pressure of his arm and the contact of his warm, strong body? What had happened to her?

Quite suddenly she knew—knew that she loved him, that she had loved him a long time, even when she thought she hated him and when she had fled from him.

She knew now why his face had haunted her in the little oasis at midday—that it was love calling to her subconsciously.

All the confusion of mind that had assailed her when they started on the homeward journey, the conflicting thoughts and contrary emotions, were explained.

But she knew herself at last and knew the

love that filled her, an overwhelming, passionate love that almost frightened her with its immensity and with the sudden hold it had laid upon her.

Love had come to her at last, she who had scorned it so fiercely.

She had given love to no one, she had thought that she could not love, that she was devoid of all natural affection, and that she would never know what love meant. But she knew now —a love of such complete surrender that she had never before conceived of it.

Her heart was given for all time to the fierce desert man who was so different from all other men whom she had met.

A lawless savage who had taken her to satisfy a passing fancy and who had treated her with merciless cruelty.

He was a brute, but she loved him, loved him for his very brutality and superb animal strength.

She was suddenly deliriously, insanely happy. She was lying against his heart, and the clasp of his arm was joy unspeakable.

She was utterly content; for the moment all life narrowed down to the immediate surroundings, and she wished childishly that they could ride so forever through eternity.

She stirred slightly, moving her head so that she could see his face showing clearly in the bright moonlight, which threw some features into high relief and left the rest in dark shadow.

She looked at him with quickening breath. He was peering intently ahead, his eyes flashing in the cold light, his brows drawn together in the characteristic heavy scowl, and the firm chin, so near her face, was pushed out more doggedly than usual.

He felt her move and glanced down.

For a moment she looked straight into his eyes, and then with a low inarticulate murmur she hid her face against him.

He did not speak, but he shifted her weight a little, drawing her closer into the curve of his arm.

It was very late when they reached the camp. Lights flashed up in the big tent and on all sides, and they were surrounded by a crowd of excited tribesmen and servants.

Diana felt stiff and giddy; a young man helped her to the door of the tent, then vanished again into the throng of men and horses.

She sank wearily onto the divan and covered her face with her hands. She was trembling with fatigue and apprehension. What would he do to her?

She asked herself the question over and over again, with shaking, soundless lips, praying for courage, nerving herself to meet him.

At last she heard his voice and, looking up, saw him standing in the doorway.

She shrank back among the soft cushions, but he took no notice of her, and, lighting a cigarette, began walking up and down the tent.

She dared not speak to him; the expression on his face was terrible.

Two soft-footed Arabs brought a hastily prepared supper. It was a ghastly meal. He never spoke or showed in any way that he was conscious of her presence.

Afterwards he resumed his restless pacing, smoking cigarette after cigarette in endless succession.

The monotonous tramp to and fro worked on Diana's nerves until she winced each time he passed her, and, huddled on the divan, she watched him continually, fascinated, fearful.

He never looked at her.

From time to time he glanced at the watch on his wrist and each time his face grew blacker. If he would only speak! His silence was worse than anything he could say.

What was he going to do? He was capable of doing anything. The suspense was torture.

Her hands grew clammy and she wrenched at the soft open collar of her riding shirt with a feeling of suffocation.

Twice Yusef came to report, and the second time the Sheik came back slowly from the door where he had been speaking to him and stopped in front of Diana, looking at her strangely.

She flung out her hands instinctively, shrinking further back among the cushions, her eyes wavering under his.

"What are you going to do to me?" she whispered involuntarily, with dry lips.

He looked at her without answering for a while, as if to prolong the torture she was enduring, and a cruel look crept into his eyes.

"That depends on what happens to Gaston," he said at length slowly.

"Gaston?" she repeated stupidly.

She had forgotten the valet; in all that had occurred since the morning she had forgotten his very existence.

"Yes—Gaston," he said sternly. "You do not seem to have thought of what might happen to him."

She sat up slowly, a puzzled look coming into her face.

"What could happen to him?" she asked wonderingly.

He dragged back the flap of the tent and pointed out into the darkness.

"Over there in the southwest, there is an old Sheik whose name is Ibraheim Omair. His tribe and mine have been at feud for generations.

"Lately I have learned that he has been venturing nearer than he has ever before dared. He hates me. To capture my personal servant would be more luck than he could have hoped for."

He dropped the flap and began walking up and down again. There was a sinister tone in his voice that made Diana suddenly comprehend the little Frenchman's peril.

Ahmed Ben Hassan was not a man to be easily alarmed on anyone's behalf. That he was anxious about Gaston was apparent, and with her knowledge of him she understood that his anxiety argued a very real danger.

"What would they do to him?" she asked shakily, with a look of horror.

The Sheik paused beside her. He looked at her curiously and the cruelty deepened in his eyes.

"Shall I tell you what they would do to him?" he said meaningly, with a terrible smile.

She gave a cry and flung her arms over her head, hiding her face.

"No! do not! Do not!" she wailed.

"Bah!" he said contemptuously. "You are squeamish."

She felt sick with the realisation of what could result to Gaston from her action. She had had no personal feeling with regard to him.

On the contrary, she liked him—he had always been respectful and attentive. She had not thought of him, the man, when she had stampeded his horse and left him on foot so far from the camp.

She had looked upon him only as a jailer, his master's deputy.

The near presence of the hostile Sheik explained many things she had not understood.

Gaston's evident desire during their ride not to go beyond a certain distance, and the special activity that had prevailed of late amongst the Sheik's immediate followers.

She had known all along the Arab's obvious affection for his French servant, and it was confirmed now by the anxiety that he did not take the trouble to conceal—so unlike his usual complete indifference to suffering or danger.

She looked at him thoughtfully.

There were still depths that she had not fathomed in his strange character. Would she ever arrive at even a distant understanding of his complex nature? There was a misty yearning in her eyes as they followed his tall figure up and down the tent.

Her newfound love longed for expression as she watched him. If she could only tell him! If she had only the right to go to him and in his arms kiss away the cruel lines from his mouth!

But she must wait until she was called, until he should choose to notice the woman whom he had taken for his pleasure, until the baser part of him had need of her again.

And when he did turn to her again the joy she would feel in his embrace would be an agony for the love that was not there.

His careless kisses would scorch her and the strength of his arms would be a mockery. But would he ever turn to her again?

If anything happened to Gaston—if what he had suggested became a fact and the servant fell a victim to the blood feud between the two tribes?

She knew he would be terribly avenged, and what would her part be? She wondered dully if he would kill her, and how. Would the long, brown fingers with their steely strength choke the life out of her?

Her hands went up to her throat mechanically.

She was trying to summon up courage to speak to him when the covering of the doorway was flung open and Gaston stood in the entrance.

"*Monseigneur*—" he stammered, and with his two hands outstretched, palm uppermost, he made an appealing gesture.

The Sheik's hand shot out and gripped the man's shoulder.

"Gaston! *Enfin, mon ami!*" he said slowly, but there was a ring in his low voice that Diana had never heard before.

For a moment the two men stared at each other, and then Ahmed Ben Hassan gave a little laugh of great relief.

"Praise be to Allah, the Merciful, the Compassionate," he murmured.

"To his name praise!" rejoined Gaston softly, then his eyes roved round the tent towards Diana, and there was no resentment in them, but only anxiety.

"*Madame* is—" He hesitated, and the Sheik cut him short.

"*Madame* is quite safe," he said drily, and pushed him gently towards the door with a few words in rapid Arabic.

He stood some time after Gaston had gone to his own quarters looking out into the night, and, when he came in, lingered unusually over closing the flap.

Diana stood hesitating. She was worn out and her long riding boots felt like lead. She was afraid to go and afraid to stay.

He seemed to be purposely ignoring her. The relief of Gaston's return was enormous, but she had still to reckon with him for her attempted flight. That he said no word about it at the moment meant nothing; she knew him too well for that.

And there was Silver Star, the finest of all his magnificent horses—she had yet to pay for his death. The strain that she had gone through since the morning was tremendous, and she could not bear much more.

His silence aggravated her breaking nerves until she felt that her control would go. He had moved over to the writing-table and was tearing the wrapping off a box of cartridges, preparatory to refilling the magazine for his revolver.

If he would not speak she must, for she could endure it no longer.

"I am sorry about Silver Star," she faltered, and even to herself her voice sounded hoarse and strange.

He did not answer, but only shrugged his shoulders as he dropped the last cartridge into its place.

The gesture and his uncompromising attitude exasperated her.

"You had better have shot me," she said bitterly.

"Perhaps. You would have been easier replaced. There are plenty of women, but Silver Star was almost unique," he retorted quickly, and she winced at the cold brutality of his tone.

A little sad smile curved her lips.

"Yet you shot your horse to get me back," she said in a barely audible voice.

He flung round with an oath.

"You little fool! Do you know so little of me yet? Do you think that I will let anything stand between me and what I want?

"Do you think that by running away from me you will make me want you less?

"By Allah! I would have found you if you had got as far as France. What I have I keep, until I tire of it—and I have not tired of you yet."

He jerked her to him, staring down at her passionately, and for a moment his face was the face of a devil.

"How shall I punish you?"

He felt the shudder he expected go through her and laughed as she shrank in his arms and hid her face. He forced her head up with merciless fingers.

"What do you hate most?—my kisses?"

With another mocking laugh he crushed his mouth to hers in a long suffocating embrace.

Then he let her go suddenly, and, blind and dizzy, she reeled from him and staggered. He caught her as she swayed and swept her into his arms.

Her head fell back against his shoulder and his face changed at the sight of her quivering features. He carried her into the adjoining room and laid her on the couch, his hands lingering as he drew them from her.

For a few moments he stood looking down with smouldering eyes on the slight, boyish figure lying on the bed, the ferocity dying out of his face.

"Take care you do not wake the devil in me again, *ma belle,*" he said sombrely.

Alone, Diana turned her face into the pillows with a moan of anguish.

Back in the desert a few hours ago, under the shining stars, when the truth had first come to her, she had thought that she was happy, but she knew now that without his love she would never be happy.

She had tasted the bitterness of his loveless kisses and she knew that a worse bitterness was to come, and she writhed at the thought of what her life with him would be.

"I love him! I love him! And I want his love more than anything in heaven and earth."

Chapter
Six

Diana was sitting on the divan in the living room of the tent, lingering over her *petit déjeuner*.

Two months had slipped away since her mad flight, since her dash for freedom that had ended in tragedy for the beautiful Silver Star and so unexpectedly for herself.

Weeks of vivid happiness that had been mixed with poignant suffering, for the perfect joy of being with him was marred by the passionate longing for his love.

Even her surroundings had taken on a new aspect, her happiness coloured everything. The beauties and attractions of the desert had multiplied a hundred times.

The wild tribesmen, with their primitive ways and savagery, had ceased to disgust her, and the free life with its constant exercise and simple routine was becoming infinitely dear to her.

The camp had been moved several times—always towards the south—and each change had been a source of greater interest.

And since the night that he had carried her back in triumph he had been kind to her—kind beyond anything that she had expected.

He had never made any reference to her flight or to the death of the horse that he had valued so highly; in that he had been generous. The episode over, he wished no further allusion to it.

But there was nothing beyond kindness. The passion that smouldered in his dark eyes often was not the love she craved.

The perpetual remembrance of those other women brought her a constant burning shame that grew stronger every day.

Shame that was only less strong than her

ardent love, and a wild jealousy that tortured her with doubts and fears, an ever-present demon of suggestion reminding her of the past when it was not she who lay in his arms, nor her lips that received his kisses.

The knowledge that the embraces she panted for had been shared by *les autres* was an open wound that would not heal.

She tried to shut her mind to the past. She knew that she was a fool to expect the abstinence of a monk in the strong, virile desert man. And she was afraid for the future.

She wanted him for herself alone, wanted his undivided love, and the fact that he was an Arab with Oriental instincts filled her with continual dread, dread of the real future, about which she never dared to think, dread of the passing of his transient desire.

She loved him so passionately, so completely, that beyond him was nothing. He was all the world.

She gave herself to him gladly, triumphantly, as she would give her life for him if need be.

But she had schooled herself to hide her love, to yield apathetically to his caresses, and to conceal the longing that possessed her.

She was afraid that the knowledge that she loved him would bring about the disaster she dreaded. The words that he had once used remained continually in her mind.

"If you loved me you would bore me, and I should have to let you go."

So she hid her love closely in her heart. It was difficult, and it hurt her to hide it from him and to assume indifference. It was difficult to remember that she must make a show of reluctance when she was longing to give unreservedly.

She looked up suddenly.

Close outside the tent the same low, vibrating baritone was singing the Kashmiri love song that she had last heard the night before she left Biskra. She sat tense, her eyes growing puzzled.

"Pale hands I loved beside the Shalimar. Where are you now? Who lies beneath your spell?"

The voice came nearer and he swept in, still singing, and came to her.

"Pale hands, pink-tipped," he sang, stopping in front of her and catching her fingers in his up to his lips, but she tore them away before he kissed them.

"You do know English!" she cried sharply, her eyes searching his.

He flung himself on the divan beside her with a laugh.

"Because I sing an English song?" he replied in French. *"Là! Là!* I heard a Spanish boy singing in *Carmen* once in Paris who did not know a word of French besides the score. He learned it parrot-like, as I learn your English songs."

She watched him light a cigarette, and her forehead wrinkled thoughtfully.

"It was you who sang outside the hotel in Biskra that night?" she asked at last, more statement than question.

"One is mad sometimes, especially when the moon is high," he replied teasingly.

"And was it you who came into my bedroom and put the blank cartridges in my revolver?"

His arm stole round her, drawing her to him, and he tilted her head up so that he could look into her eyes.

"Do you think that I would have allowed anybody else to go to your room at night?—I, an Arab, when I meant you for myself?"

"You were so sure?"

He laughed softly, as if the suggestion that any plan of his could be liable to miscarriage amused him infinitely, and the smouldering passion flamed up in his dark eyes.

He strained her to him hungrily, as if her slim body lying against his had awakened the sleeping fires within him. She struggled against the pressure of his arm, averting her head.

"Always cold?" he chided. "Kiss me, little piece of ice."

She longed to, and it almost broke her heart to persevere in her efforts to repel him.

A wild desire seized her to tell him that she loved him, to make an end once and for all of the misery of doubt and fear that was sapping her strength from her, and abide by the issue.

But the spark of hope that lived in her heart gave her courage, and she fought down the burning words that sought utterance, forcing indifference into her eyes and a mutinous pout to her lips.

His black brows drew together slowly.

"Still disobedient? You said you would obey me. I loathe the English, but I thought their word—"

She interrupted him with a quick gesture, and, turning her face to his, for the first time kissed him voluntarily, brushing his tanned cheek with swift, cold lips.

He laughed disdainfully.

"Bon Dieu! Has the hot sun of the desert taught you no better than that? Have you learned so little from me? Has the vile climate of your detestable country frozen you? Or is there some man in England who has the power to turn you from a statue to a woman?"

She clenched her hands with the pain of his words.

"There is no one," she muttered, "but I—I don't feel like that."

"You had better learn," he said thickly. "I am tired of holding an icicle in my arms."

Sweeping her completely into his masterful grasp, he covered her face with fierce, burning kisses.

And for the first time she surrendered to him wholly, clinging to him passionately, and giving him kiss for kiss with an absolute abandon of all resistance.

At last he let her go, panting and breathless, and leapt up, drawing his hand across his eyes.

"You go to my head, Diana."

With a laugh that was half anger, he

shrugged his shoulders and moved across the tent to the chest where the spare arms were kept. Unlocking it, he took out a revolver and began to clean it.

She looked at him bewildered. What had he meant? How could she reconcile what he said with the advice that he had given her before? Was he totally inconsistent?

Did he, after all, want the satisfaction of knowing that he had made her love him—of flattering himself on the power that he exercised over her?

Did he care that he was able to torture her heart with a refinement of cruelty that took all and gave nothing?

Did he wish her to crawl abjectly to his feet to give him the pleasure of spurning her contemptuously, or was it only that he wanted her senses merely to respond to his ardent Eastern temperament?

Her face grew hot and ashamed. She knew the fiery nature that was hidden under his impassive exterior and the control he exercised over himself.

She sighed again wearily. If she could but make him and keep him happy.

She knelt up suddenly on the cushions of the divan.

"Why do you hate the English so bitterly, *Monseigneur?*"

She had dropped almost unconsciously into Gaston's mode of address some time before; it was often awkward to give him no name. She shrank from using his own; and the title fitted him.

He looked up from his work, and, gathering the materials together, brought them over to the divan.

"Light me a cigarette, *chèrie*, my hands are busy," he replied irrelevantly.

She complied with a little laugh.

"You haven't answered my question."

He polished the gleaming little weapon in his hand for some time without speaking.

"*Ma petite* Diana, your lips are of an adorable redness and your voice is music in my ears, but—I detest questions. They bore me to a point of exasperation."

He started humming the Kashmiri Song again.

She knew him well enough to know that all questions did not bore him, but that she must have touched some point connected with the past of which she was ignorant that affected him, and to prove her knowledge she asked another question.

"Why do you sing? You have never sung before."

He looked at her with a smile of amusement at her pertinacity.

"Inquisitive one! I sing because I am glad. Because my friend is coming."

"Your friend?"

"Yes, by Allah! The best friend a man ever had: Raoul de Saint Hubert."

She flashed a look at the bookcase with a jerk of her head, and he nodded.

"Coming here?" she queried, and the dismay she felt sounded in her voice.

He frowned in quick annoyance at her tone. "Why not?" he said haughtily.

"No reason," she murmured, sinking down among the cushions again and picking up the magazine from the floor.

The advent of a stranger—a European—was a shock, but she felt that the Sheik's eyes were on her and she determined to show no feeling in his presence.

"What time will you be ready to ride?" she asked indifferently, with a simulated yawn, flitting over the pages.

"I can't ride with you today. I am going to meet Saint Hubert. His courier only came an hour ago. It is two years since I have seen him."

Diana slipped off the couch and went to the open doorway. A detachment of men were already waiting for him, and, close by the tent, Shaitan of the ugly temper was biting and fidgeting in the hands of the grooms.

She scowled at the beautiful, wicked creature's flat-laid ears and rolling eyes. She would have backed him fearlessly herself if the Sheik had let her, but she was nervous for him every time he rode the vicious beast.

No one but the Sheik could manage him, and though she knew that he had perfect mastery over the horse, she never lost the feeling of nervousness.

"It makes my head ache to stay in all day.

May Gaston not ride with me?" she asked diffidently, her eyes anywhere but on his face.

He had not allowed her to ride with anyone except himself since her attempted escape, and to her tentative suggestions that the rides with the valet might be resumed he had given a prompt refusal.

He hesitated now, and she was afraid he was going to refuse again, and she looked up wistfully.

"Please, *Monseigneur*," she whispered humbly.

He looked at her for a moment with his chin squarer than usual.

"Are you going to run away again?" he asked bluntly.

Her eyes filled slowly with tears, and she turned her head away to hide them.

"No, I am not going to run away again," she said very low.

"Very well, I will tell him. He will be delighted, *le bon* Gaston. He is your very willing slave in spite of the trick you played him. He has a beautiful nature, *le pauvre diable*. He is not an Arab, eh, little Diana?"

The mocking smile was back in his eyes as he turned her face to his in the usual peremptory way.

Then he held out the revolver he had been cleaning with sudden seriousness.

"I want you to carry this always now when you ride. Ibraheim Omair is still in the neighbourhood."

She looked at it blankly.

"But—" she stammered.

He knew what was in her mind, and he stooped and kissed her lightly.

"I trust you," he said quietly.

She watched him mount and ride away.

His horsemanship was superb and her eyes glowed as they followed him.

She went back into the tent and slipped the revolver into the holster he had left lying on a stool, and, tucking it and Saint Hubert's novel, which she took from the bookcase, under her arm, she went into the bedroom.

She threw herself on the bed to laze away the morning and to try to picture the author from the book he had written.

She hated him in advance; she was jealous of him and of his coming. The Sheik's sudden new tenderness had given rise to a hope she hardly dared allow herself to dwell upon.

She turned to the title-page and closely studied the pencilled scrawl: *Souvenir de Raoul.* It did not look like the handwriting of a small-minded man, but handwriting was nothing to go by, she argued obstinately.

She turned the pages, dipping here and there, finally forgetting the author altogether in the book. It was a wonderful story of a man's love and faithfulness, and Diana pushed it aside at last with a very bitter sigh.

Things happened so in books. In real life they happened very differently. She looked round the room with pain-filled eyes, at the medley of her own and the Sheik's belongings.

Then she looked at the pillow beside her where his head rested every night. She stooped and kissed it with a little quivering breath.

"Ahmed. Oh, *Monseigneur!*" she murmured longingly.

With an impatient jerk of the head, she sprang up and dragged on her boots. She pulled a soft felt hat down over her eyes and picked up the revolver the Sheik had given her.

Gaston's face lit up with genuine pleasure when she came out to the horses.

The horse that she rode always now was pure white, not so fast as Silver Star and very tricky, called The Dancer, from a nervous habit of dancing on his hind legs at starting and stopping, like a circus horse.

He was difficult to mount, and edged away shyly as Diana tried to get her foot into the stirrup. But she swung up at last, and by the time The Dancer had finished his display of *haute école* Gaston was mounted.

She wanted exercise primarily, hard physical exercise that would tire her out and keep her mind occupied and prevent her from thinking, and the horse she rode supplied both needs.

After a while she reined in her horse and waved to Gaston to come alongside.

"Tell me of this *Vicomte* de Saint Hubert who is coming. You know him, I suppose, as you have been so long with *Monseigneur?*"

Gaston smiled.

"I knew him before *Monseigneur* did. I was born on the estate of *Monsieur le Comte* de Saint Hubert, the father of *Monsieur le Vicomte*. I and my twin brother, Henri.

"We both went into *Monsieur le Comte*'s training stables, and then after our time in the Cavalry Henri became valet to *Monsieur le Vicomte*, and I came to *Monseigneur*."

Diana decided against any more questions.

She coaxed her nervous mount close beside his steadier companion, and, thrusting his bridle and her hat into Gaston's hands, she slipped to the ground and walked away a little distance to the top of a small mound.

She sat down on the summit with her back to the horses and her arms clasped round her knees.

How, she asked herself, could she bear to meet one of her own order in the position in which she was? She, who had been proud Diana Mayo and now—the mistress of an Arab Sheik.

She laid her face on her knees with a shudder. The ordeal before her cut like a knife into her heart.

A discreet cough from Gaston warned her that time was flying.

She went back to the horses slowly with white face and compressed lips.

There was the usual trouble in mounting, and her strained nerves made her impatient with The Dancer's idiosyncrasies, and she checked him sharply, making him rear dangerously.

"Careful, *Madame*," cried Gaston warningly.

"For whom—me or *Monseigneur*'s horse?" she retorted bitterly, and spurred the horse viciously, making him break into a headlong gallop.

The horse's nerves, like her own, were on edge, and he pulled badly, his smooth satiny neck growing dark and steamed with sweat.

Diana needed all her knowledge to control him, and she began to wonder if when they came to the camp she would be able to stop him.

As they neared the tents she saw the Sheik standing outside his, with a tall, thin man beside him.

She had only a glimpse of dark hair and a close-cut beard as she shot past, unable to pull up The Dancer.

But just beyond the tent, with the reins cutting into her hands, she managed to haul him round and bring him back. The Sheik came forward and she slid down.

"Diana, the *Vicomte* de Saint Hubert waits to be presented to you."

She drew herself up and the colour that had come into her face drained out of it again.

Slowly she glanced up at the man standing before her, and looked straight into the most sympathetic eyes that her own sad, defiant ones had ever seen.

Only for a moment, then he bowed with a conventional murmur that was barely audible.

His lack of words gave her courage.

"*Monsieur*," she said coldly in response to

his greeting, then turned to the Sheik without looking at him.

"The Dancer has behaved abominably!"

Then she vanished into the tent without a further look at anyone.

It was late, but she lingered over her bath and changed with slow reluctance into the green dress that the Sheik preferred—a concession that she despised herself for making. She had taken up the jade necklace when he joined her.

He turned her to him roughly, with his hands on her shoulders, and the merciless pressure of his fingers was indication enough without the black scowl on his face that he was angry.

"You are not very cordial to my guest."

"Is it required of a slave to be cordial towards her master's friends?" she replied in a stifled voice.

"What is required is obedience to my wishes," he said harshly.

"And is it your wish that I should please this Frenchman?"

"It is my wish."

"If I were a woman of your own race—" she began bitterly, but he interrupted her.

"If you were a woman of my own race there would be no question of it," he said coldly. "You would be for the eyes of no other man than me. But since you are not—"

He broke off with an enigmatical jerk of the head.

"Since I am not you are less merciful than if

I were," she cried miserably. "I could wish that I were an Arab woman."

"I doubt it," he said grimly. "The life of an Arab woman would hardly be to your taste. We teach our women obedience with a whip."

"Why have you changed so since this morning," she whispered, "when you told me that you trusted no one to climb to my balcony in the hotel but yourself? Are you not an Arab now as then? Have I become of so little value to you that you are not even jealous anymore?"

"I can trust my friend, and—I do not propose to share you with him," he said brutally.

She winced as if he had struck her, and hid her face in her hands with a low cry.

His fingers gripped her shoulders cruelly.

"You will do as I wish?"

The words were a question, but the intonation was a command.

"I have no choice," she murmured faintly.

His hands dropped to his sides and he turned to leave the room, but she caught his arm.

"*Monseigneur!* Have you no pity? Will you not spare me this ordeal?"

He made a gesture of refusal.

"You exaggerate," he said impatiently, brushin her hand from his arm.

"If you will be merciful this once—" she pleaded breathlessly, but he cut her short with a fierce oath.

"If?" he echoed. "Do you make bargains with me? Have you so much yet to learn?"

She looked at him with a little weary sigh.

She could not bear his anger. She longed so desperately for happiness, and she loved him so passionately, so utterly, that she was content to give up everything to his will.

If she could only get back the man of the last few weeks, if she had not angered him too far.

She was at his feet, tamed thoroughly at last, all her proud, angry self-will swamped in the love that was consuming her with an intensity that was an agony.

Love was a bitter pain, a torment that was almost unendurable, a happiness that mocked her with its hollowness, a misery that tortured her with visions of what might have been.

She went to him slowly, and he turned to her abruptly.

"Well?"

His voice was hard and uncompromising, and the flash of his eyes was like the tiger's in the Indian jungle.

She set her teeth to keep down the old paralysing fear.

"I will do what you want. I will do anything you want, only be kind to me, Ahmed," she whispered unsteadily.

She had never called him by his name before; she did not even know that she had done so now, but at the sound of it a curious look crossed his face, and he drew her into his arms with hands that were as gentle as they had been cruel before.

She let him lift her face to his, and met his

searching gaze bravely. Holding her eyes with the mesmerism that he could exert when he chose, he read in her face her final surrender, and knew that while it pleased him to keep her he had broken her utterly to his hand.

A strange expression grew in his eyes as they travelled slowly over her. In his strong grasp she was like a fragile reed that he could crush without an effort.

Yet for four months she had fought him, matching his determination with a courage that had won his admiration even while it had exasperated him.

He knew that she feared him, he had seen terror leap into her flickering eyes when she had defied him most.

Her defiance and her hatred, which had piqued him by contrast with the fawning adulation to which he had been accustomed and which had wearied him infinitely, had provoked in him a fixed resolve to master her.

Before he tired of her she must yield her will to him absolutely.

And tonight he knew that the last struggle had been made, that she would never oppose him again, that she was clay in his hands to do with as he would.

And the knowledge that he had won gave him no feeling of exultation. Instead a vague, indefinite sense of irritation swept over him and made him swear softly under his breath.

The satisfaction he had expected in his triumph was lacking and the unaccountable dissatisfaction that filled him seemed inexplicable. He did not understand himself, and he looked down at her again with a touch of impatience.

She was very lovely, he thought, with a strange new appreciation of the beauty he had appropriated, and very womanly in the soft, clinging green dress.

The slim, boyish figure that rode with him had a charm all its own, but it was the woman in her that sent the hot blood racing through his veins and made his heart beat as it was beating now.

His eyes lingered a moment on her bright curls, on her dark-fringed, pleading eyes, and on her bare neck, startlingly white against the jade green of her gown, then he put her from him.

"*Va*," he said gently, "*depêche-toi*."

She looked after him as he went through the curtains with a long, sobbing sigh. She was paying a heavy price for her happiness, but nothing mattered now that he was not angry anymore.

She turned to the glass suddenly and wrenched the silk folds off her shoulder. She looked at the marks of his fingers on the delicate skin with a twist of the lips, then shut her eyes with a little gasp and hid her bruised arm hastily, her mouth quivering.

"If he killed me he could not kill my love," she murmured, with a little pitiful smile.

The men were waiting for her, and with a murmured apology for her lateness she took her place.

Ahmed Ben Hassan and his guest resumed the conversation that her entrance had interrupted.

She glanced at the Sheik covertly. There was a look on his face that she had never seen and a ring in his voice that was different even from the tone she had heard when Gaston had come back on the night of her flight.

That had been relief and the affection of a man for a valued servant; this was the deep affection of a man for the one chosen friend, the love passing the love of women.

The jealousy she had felt in the morning welled up uncontrollably.

She looked from the Sheik to the man who was absorbing all his attention.

And as she looked her eyes met his. A smile that was extraordinarily sweet and half-sad lit up his face.

"Is it permitted to admire *Madame*'s horsemanship?" he asked, with a little bow.

Diana coloured faintly and twisted the jade necklace round her fingers nervously.

"It is nothing," she said, with a shy smile that his sympathetic personality evoked in spite of herself. "With The Dancer it is all foolishness and not vice. It is an education to ride *Monseigneur*'s horses, *Monsieur*."

"It is a strain to the nerves to ride *beside* some of them," replied the *Vicomte* pointedly.

Diana laughed with pure amusement. The man whose coming she had loathed was making the dreaded ordeal very easy for her.

"I sympathise, *Monsieur*. Was Shaitan very vile?"

"If *Monsieur* de Saint Hubert is trying to suggest to you that he suffers from nerves, Diana," broke in the Sheik, with a laugh, "disabuse yourself at once. He has none."

Saint Hubert turned to him with a quick smile.

"*Et toi*, Ahmed, eh? Do you remember——?" And he plunged into a flood of reminiscences that lasted until the end of dinner.

The *Vicomte* had brought with him a pile of newspapers and magazines, and Diana curled up on the divan with an armful, hungry for news, but, somehow, as she dipped into the batch of papers her interest waned.

The two men had forgotten her presence with the accumulated conversation of two years.

She was thankful to be left alone, happy for the rare chance of studying the beloved face unnoticed.

It was seldom that she had the opportunity, for when they were alone she was afraid to look at him much lest her secret should be betrayed in her eyes. But she looked at him now unobserved, with passionate longing.

She was so intent that she did not notice Gaston come in until he seemed suddenly to appear from nowhere beside his master. He murmured something softly and the Sheik got up. He turned to Saint Hubert.

"Trouble with one of the horses. Will you come? It may interest you."

They went out together, leaving her alone, and she slipped away to the inner room.

In half an hour they came back, and for a few minutes longer stayed chattering, then the *Vicomte* yawned and held out his watch with a laugh.

The Sheik went with him to his tent and sat down on the side of his guest's camp-bed. Saint Hubert dismissed the waiting Henri with a nod and started to undress silently.

The flow of talk and ready laughter seemed to have deserted him, and he frowned as he wrenched his things off with nervous irritability.

The Sheik watched him for a while, and then took the cigarette out of his mouth with a faint smile.

"Eh bien! Raoul, say it," he said quietly.

Saint Hubert swung round.

"You might have spared her," he cried.

"What?"

"What? Good God, man! Me!"

The Sheik flicked the ash from his cigarette with a gesture of indifference.

"Your courier was delayed, he only came this morning. It was too late then to make other arrangements."

"It is abominable," Saint Hubert burst out. "You go too far, Ahmed."

The Sheik laughed cynically.

"What do you expect of a savage? When an Arab sees a woman that he wants he takes her. I only follow the customs of my people."

Saint Hubert clicked his tongue impatiently.

"Your people!—which people?" he asked in a low voice.

The Sheik sprang to his feet with flashing eyes, his hand dropping heavily on Saint Hubert's shoulder.

"Stop, Raoul! Not even from you—!" he cried passionately.

Then he broke off abruptly, and the anger died out of his face.

He sat down again quietly, with a little amused laugh.

"Why this sudden access of morality, *mon ami?* You know me and the life I lead. You have seen women in my camp before now."

Saint Hubert dismissed the remark with a contemptuous wave of the hand.

"There is no comparison. You know it as well as I," he said succinctly. "She is English, surely that is reason enough."

"You ask me, *me,* to spare a woman because she is English? My good Raoul, you amuse me," replied the Sheik, with an ugly sneer.

"Where did you see her?" asked Saint Hubert curiously.

"In the streets of Biskra, for five minutes, four months ago."

"You love her?"

"Have I ever loved a woman? And this woman is English," he said in a voice as hard as steel.

"If you loved her you would not care for her nationality."

"By Allah! Her cursed race sticks in my throat. But for that—"

He shrugged his shoulders impatiently and got up from the bed on which he was sitting.

"Let her go then," said Saint Hubert quickly. "I can take her back to Biskra."

The Sheik turned to him slowly, a sudden flame of fierce jealousy leaping into his eyes.

"Has she bewitched you, too? Do you want her for yourself, Raoul?"

His voice was as low as ever, but there was a dangerous ring in it. Saint Hubert flung his hands out in a gesture of despair.

"Ahmed! Are you mad? Are you going to quarrel with me after all these years on such a pretext? *Bon Dieu!* What do you take me for? There has been too much in our lives together ever to let a woman come between us."

"Forgive me, Raoul. You know my devilish temper," muttered the Sheik, and for a moment his hand rested on Saint Hubert's arm.

"You have not answered me, Ahmed."

The Sheik turned away.

"She is content," he said evasively.

"She has courage," amended the *Vicomte* significantly.

"As you say, she has courage," agreed the Sheik, without a particle of expression in his voice.

"Bon sang—" quoted Saint Hubert softly.

The Sheik swung round quickly.

"How did you know she has good blood in her?"

"It is very evident," replied Saint Hubert drily.

"That is not what you mean. What do you know?"

The *Vicomte* shrugged his shoulders, and, going to his suitcase, took from it an English illustrated paper, and opening it at the central page handed it to the Sheik silently.

Ahmed Ben Hassan moved closer to the hanging lamp so that the light fell directly on the paper in his hands.

There were two large full-length photographs of Diana, one in evening dress and the other as the *Vicomte* had first seen her, in riding breeches and short jacket, her hat and whip lying at her feet, and the bridle of the horse that was standing beside her over her arm.

Under the photograph was written:

Miss Diana Mayo, whose protracted journey in the desert, is causing anxiety to a large circle of friends.

Miss Mayo left Biskra under the guidance of a reputable caravan leader four months ago, with the intention of journeying for four weeks in the desert and returning to Oran.

Since the first camp nothing has been heard of Miss Mayo or her caravan. Further anxiety is occasioned by the fact that considerable unrest is reported amongst the tribes in the locality towards which Miss Mayo was travelling.

Her brother, Sir Aubrey Mayo, who is detained in America as the result of an accident, is in constant cable communication with the French authorities.

Miss Mayo is a well-known sportswoman and has travelled widely.

For a long time the Sheik studied the photographs silently, then with slow deliberation he tore the page out of the paper and rolled it up.

"With your permission," he said coolly.

He held it over the flame of the little lamp by the bedside. He held it until the burning paper charred to nothing in his hand and then flicked the ashes from his long fingers.

"What are you going to do?" asked Saint Hubert pointedly.

"I? Nothing! The French authorities have too many affairs on hand to prosecute enquiries in my direction. Besides, they are not responsible. *Mademoiselle* Mayo was warned of the risks she ran before she left Biskra. She chose to take the risks, *et voilà!*"

"Will nothing make you change your mind?"

"I am not given to changing my mind. You know that. And besides, why should I? As I told you before, she is content."

Saint Hubert looked him full in the face.

"Content! Cowed is the better word, Ahmed."

The Sheik laughed softly.

"You flatter me, Raoul. Do not let us speak any more about it. It is an unfortunate *contretemps,* and I regret that it distresses you. But this can make no difference to our friendship, *mon ami;* that is too big a thing to break down over a difference of opinion.

"You are a French nobleman, and I am an uncivilised Arab. We cannot see things in the same way."

"You could, but you will not, Ahmed," replied the *Vicomte,* with an accent of regret. "It is not worthy of you."

He paused and then looked up again with a little crooked smile and a shrug of defeat.

"Nothing can ever make any difference with us, Ahmed. I can disagree with you, but I can't wipe out the recollection of the last twenty years."

A few minutes later the Sheik left him and went into his own tent.

The divan where Diana had been sitting was strewn with magazines, and the imprint of her slender body still showed in the soft, heaped-up cushions, and a tiny, lace-edged handkerchief peeped out under one of them.

He picked it up and looked at it curiously, and his forehead contracted slowly in the heavy black scowl.

He turned his burning eyes towards the curtains that divided the rooms. Saint Hubert's words rang in his ears.

"English!" he muttered with a terrible oath. "And I have made her suffer as I swore any of that damned race should if they fell into my hands. Merciful Allah! Why does it give me so little pleasure?"

Chapter Seven

Diana came into the living room about a week after the arrival of the *Vicomte* de Saint Hubert. She saw him sitting at the little writing-table.

It was the first time that they had chanced to

be alone, and she hesitated with a sudden shyness. But Saint Hubert had heard the rustle of the curtain, and he sprang to his feet.

"Your pardon, *Madame*. Do I disturb you? Tell me if I am in the way."

"I thought you had gone with *Monseigneur*."

"I had some work to do—some notes that I wanted to transcribe before I forgot myself what they meant."

"Is it another novel?" Diana asked shyly, indicating the steadily increasing pile of manuscript.

He turned on his chair, and smiled at her as she curled up on the divan with Kopec, who had followed her into the tent.

"No, *Madame*. Something more serious this time. It is a history of this very curious tribe of Ahmed's. They are different in so many ways from ordinary Arabs."

Diana studied him curiously as he bent over his work.

"I have read your books, *Monsieur*—all that *Monseigneur* has here," she said.

He gave a little bow with a few murmured words that she did not catch.

And then Henri came in quickly.

"*Monsieur le Vicomte!* Will you come? There has been an accident."

With a cry that Saint Hubert never forgot, Diana leapt to her feet, her face colourless, and her lips framed the word "Ahmed," though no sound came from them.

She was shaking all over, and the *Vicomte* put his arm round her instinctively.

"What is it, Henri?" he said sharply.

"One of the men, *Monsieur le Vicomte*. His gun burst, and his hand is shattered."

Saint Hubert nodded curtly towards the door and turned his attention to Diana. She sank down on the divan.

"Forgive me," she murmured. "It is stupid of me, but he is riding that brute Shaitan today. I am always nervous. Please go. I will come in a minute."

Diana sat quite still after he had gone until the nervous shuddering ceased. She brushed her hand across her eyes with a gasp of relief, and went out into the bright sunlight.

The wounded man was sitting, holding up his hand for Saint Hubert's ministrations. In response to Diana's smile and cheery word he grinned sheepishly with a roll of his fine eyes.

Saint Hubert looked up quickly.

"It's not a pleasant sight," he said doubtfully.

"I don't mind. Let me hold that," she said quietly, rolling up her sleeves and taking a crimson-spattered basin from Henri.

She watched the *Vicomte*'s skilful treatment of the maimed hand with interest. There was a precision in his movements and a deft touch that indicated both knowledge and practice.

"You are a doctor?"

"Yes," he said, without looking up from his

work, "I studied when I was a young man and passed all the necessary examinations. It is indispensable when one travels as I do. I have found it invaluable."

He finished adjusting the bandages and stood up.

"Will he do all right now?" asked Diana anxiously.

"I think so. The thumb is gone, as you saw, but I think I can save the rest of the hand. I will watch him carefully, but these men of Ahmed's are in such excellent condition that I do not think there will be any trouble."

"I am going to ride," said Diana, turning away. "It is rather late, but there is just time. Will you come?"

"I should like to, but I ought to keep an eye on Selim," he said quietly.

"If I am late don't wait for me. Tell Henri to give you your lunch," she called out.

He watched her ride away, with Gaston a few paces behind and followed by the escort of six men that the Sheik had lately insisted upon.

She thought of the Sheik. His mood, since the coming of Saint Hubert, had been the coldest. The weeks of happiness that had gone before had developed the intimacy between them almost into a feeling of camaraderie.

But since the morning of Raoul's arrival his caresses had been careless and infrequent, and his indifference so great that she had wondered miserably if the flame of his passion for her was burning out, and if this was the end.

Her heart tightened at the thought of his indifference. It hurt so. This morning he had left her without a word when he had gone out into the early dawn, and she was hungry for the kisses he withheld.

She had yielded up everything to him, he dominated her wholly. Her imperious will had bent before his greater determination, and his mastery over her had provoked a love that craved recompense.

She lived only for him and for the hope of his love, engulfed in the passion that enthralled her.

Her surrender had been no common one. The feminine weakness that she had despised and fought against had triumphed over her unexpectedly with humiliating thoroughness.

Today she was almost desperate. His callousness of the morning had wounded her deeply, and a wave of rebellion welled up in her.

She would not be thrown aside without making any effort to fight for his love. She would use every art that her beauty and her woman's instinct gave her.

Her cheeks burned as she thought of the role she was setting herself. She would be no better than "those others" whose remembrances still made her shiver.

Gaston spurred to Diana's side.

"Will *Madame* please to turn?" he said respectfully. "It is late and it is not safe riding amongst these slopes. One cannot see what is coming and I am afraid."

"Afraid, Gaston?" she rallied, laughing.

"For you, *Madame,*" he answered gravely.

She reined in The Dancer as she spoke, but it was too late. Even as she turned her horse's head, innumerable Arabs seemed to spring up on all sides of them.

Before she realised what was happening her escort flashed past and wheeled in behind her, shooting steadily at the horde of men who poured in upon them.

With a groan, Gaston seized her bridle and urged the horses back in the direction from which they had come. The noise was deafening. Bullets began to whizz past her.

Gaston tucked his reins under his knee, and with one hand grasping The Dancer's bridle and his revolver in the other, rode looking back over his shoulder.

Diana too glanced behind her, and mechanically her fingers closed over the shining little weapon that the Sheik had given her the previous week.

She saw with a sudden sickening the six men who had formed her escort beaten back by the superior numbers that enclosed them on every side.

Already two were down and the rest were on foot, and as she watched they were swallowed up in the mass of men that poured over them, and at the same time a party of about twenty horsemen detached themselves from the main body and galloped towards her and Gaston.

She seized his arm.

"Can't we do something? Can't we help them? We can't leave them like that," she gasped, wrenching the revolver from the holster at her waist.

"No, no, *Madame*, it is impossible. It is a hundred to six. You must think of yourself. Go on, *Madame*. For God's sake, ride on. We may have a chance."

He loosed her bridle and dropped behind her, interposing himself between her and the pursuing Arabs. A fierce yelling and a hail of bullets that went wide made Diana turn her head as she crouched low in the saddle.

She realised the meaning of Gaston's tactics and checked her horse deliberately.

"I won't go first. You must ride with me," she cried, wincing as a bullet went close by her.

"Mon Dieu! What are you stopping for? Do you think I can face *Monseigneur* if anything happens to you, *Madame?"* replied Gaston fiercely. "Do as I tell you. Go on!"

Fear roughened his voice. He looked back and his face grew grey. For himself he had no fear, but for the girl beside him he dared not even think.

They were Ibraheim Omair's men who had trapped them, and he cursed his folly in allowing

Diana to come so far. Yet it had seemed safe enough.

This must be a sudden tentative raid which had met with unlooked-for success.

The bait would be too tempting to allow of any slackening on the part of the raiders.

The white woman, who was Ahmed Ben Hassan's latest toy, and his servant, whom he was known to value so highly, would be a prize that would not be lightly let go. For himself it would be probably torture, certainly death, and for her—!

He set his teeth as he looked at her. He would kill her himself before it came to that. And as he looked she turned her head, and met his agonised eyes for a moment, smiling bravely.

He had refrained up till now from shooting, trying to reserve his ammunition for a last resource, but he saw that he must delay no longer. He fired slowly and steadily, picking his men with careful precision.

It was a forlorn hope, but by checking the leaders even for a few moments he might gain time.

Diana was shooting too. She fired rapidly, emptying her revolver, and she had just reloaded when The Dancer stumbled, recovered himself for a few steps, and then lurched slowly over onto his side, blood pouring from his mouth.

Diana sprang clear, and in a moment Gaston was beside her, thrusting her behind him, shielding her with his own body, and firing steadily at the oncoming Arabs.

The same feeling of unreality that she had experienced once before the first day in the Sheik's camp came over her. Any minute might mean death for one or the other or both of them, and with an instinctive movement she pressed closer to Gaston.

They were both silent, there seemed nothing to say. The valet's left hand clenched over hers at the involuntary appeal for companionship that she made, and she felt it contract as a bullet gashed his forehead, blinding him for a moment with the blood that dripped into his eyes.

He let go of her hand to brush his arm across his face, and as he did so the Arabs with suddenly renewed shouting bore down upon them.

Gaston turned sharply and Diana read his purpose in the horror in his eyes. She held up her head with a little nod, and the same brave smile on her white lips.

"Please," she whispered, "quickly!"

A spasm crossed his face.

"Turn your head," he muttered desperately. "I cannot do it if you—"

There was a rattle of shots, and with a gasp he crumpled against her. For a moment it was pandemonium.

Standing over Gaston's body, she fired her last shot and flung the empty revolver in the face of a man who sprang forward to seize her.

151

She turned with a desperate hope of reaching Gaston's horse. Then she was conscious of a crushing blow on her head, the ground heaved up under her feet, everything went black before her eyes, and without a sound she fell senseless.

* * *

Late in the afternoon Saint Hubert was still writing in the big tent.

He had forgotten the time, forgotten to be surprised at Diana's continued absence, immersed in the interesting subject he was dealing with, and not realising the significance of her delayed return.

He was too engrossed to notice the usual noise in the camp that heralded the Sheik's arrival, and he looked up with a start when Ahmed Ben Hassan swept in. The Sheik's dark eyes glanced sombrely round the tent and without a word he went through into the inner room. In a moment he came back.

"Where is Diana?"

Saint Hubert got up, puzzled at his tone. He looked at his watch.

"She went for a ride this morning. *Dieu!* I had no idea it was so late."

"This morning!—and not back yet?" repeated the Sheik slowly. "What time this morning?"

"About ten, I think," replied Saint Hubert uneasily. "I'm not sure. I didn't look. There was an accident, and she delayed to watch me tie up one

of your foolish children who had been playing
with a worthless gun."

The Sheik moved over to the doorway.

"She had an escort?" he asked curtly.

"Yes."

Ahmed Ben Hassan's face hardened and the
heavy scowl contracted his black brows. Had she
all these weeks been tricking him—feigning a content she did not feel, lulling his suspicions to en-
able her to seize another opportunity to attempt
to get away?

For a moment his face grew dark, then he
put the thought from him. He trusted her. Only a
week before she had given him her word, and he
knew she would not lie to him. And besides, the
thing was impossible.

Gaston would never be caught napping a
second time, and there were also the six men who
formed her guard.

She would never be able to escape the vigilance of seven men. But it was the trust he had
in her that weighed most with him. He had never
trusted a woman before, but this woman had been
different.

The emotion that this girl's uncommon beauty
and slender boyishness had aroused in him had
not diminished during the months she had been
living in his camp. Her varying moods, her antag-
onism, her fits of furious rage, and, lastly, her
unexpected surrender had kept his interest alive.

He had grown accustomed to her. He had

come to look forward with a vague, indefinite pleasure, on returning from his long expeditions, to seeing the dainty little figure curled up among the cushions on the big divan.

Her presence seemed to pervade the atmosphere of the whole tent, changing it utterly. She had become necessary to him as he had never believed it possible that a woman could be.

And with the change that she had made in his camp there had come a change in himself alone.

For the first time a shadow had risen between him and the man whose friendship had meant everything to him. He realised that since the night of Raoul's arrival he had been seething with insensate jealousy.

He had relied on the Western tendencies that prompted him to carry off the difficult situation, but his ingrained Orientalism had broken through the superficial veneer. He was jealous of every word, of every look she gave Saint Hubert.

He went out under the awning and clapped his hands, and a servant answered the summons almost immediately. He gave an order and waited, his hands thrust into the folds of his waist-cloth.

Saint Hubert joined him.

"What do you think?" he asked, with a touch of diffidence.

"I don't know what to think," replied the Sheik shortly.

"But is there any real danger?"

"There is always danger in the desert, particularly when that devil is abroad." He motioned to the south with an impatient jerk of his head.

Saint Hubert's breath whistled sharply between his teeth.

"My God! You don't imagine—"

But the Sheik only shrugged his shoulders and turned to Yusef, who had come up with half a dozen men. There was a rapid interchange of questions and answers, some brief orders, and the men hurried away in different directions, while Ahmed Ben Hassan turned again to Saint Hubert.

"They were seen by three of the southern patrols this morning but of course it was nobody's business to find out if they had come back or not. I will start at once—in about ten minutes. You will come with me?"

He paused a moment.

" Good! I have sent for re-enforcements, who are to follow us if we are not back in twelve hours."

His voice was expressionless, and only Raoul de Saint Hubert could appreciate the significance of the fleeting look that crossed his face as he went back into the tent.

The short twilight had gone and a brilliant moon shone high in the heavens, illuminating the surrounding country with a clear white light. They had left the level country and were in amongst the long, successive ranges of undulating ground.

At the bottom of one of the slopes the Sheik pulled up suddenly with a low, hissing exclamation. A white shape was lying face downwards, spread-eagled on the sand, and at their approach two lean, slinking forms cantered away into the night.

The Sheik and Henri reached the still figure simultaneously and Saint Hubert almost as quickly. He made a hurried examination.

The bullet that had stunned Gaston had glanced off, leaving an ugly cut, and others that had hit him at the same time had ploughed through his shoulder, breaking the bone and causing besides wounds that had bled freely.

He had staggered more than a mile before he had fainted again from the loss of blood. He came to under Saint Hubert's handling, and lifted his heavy eyes to the Sheik, who was kneeling beside him.

*"Monseigneur—Madame—*Ibraheim Omair," he whispered weakly, and relapsed into unconsciousness.

For a moment the Sheik's eyes met Raoul's across his body, and then Ahmed Ben Hassan rose to his feet.

"Be as quick as you can," he said.

He went back to his horse, his fingers mechanically searching for and lighting a cigarette, his eyes fixed unseeingly on the group round Gaston.

The valet's broken words had confirmed the fear that he had striven to crush since he had first discovered Diana's absence.

He had only seen Ibraheim Omair once, when,

ten years before, he had gone to a meeting of the more powerful Chiefs at Algiers.

But the memory of the robber Sheik remained with him always, and the recollection of his bloated, vicious face and gross, unwieldy body rose clearly before him now.

Ibraheim Omair and the slender daintiness that he had prized so lightly. Diana!

His senseless jealousy and the rage provoked by Raoul's outspoken criticism had recoiled on the innocent cause. She, not Saint Hubert, had felt the brunt of his anger.

In the innate cruelty of his nature it had given him a subtle pleasure to watch the bewilderment, alternating with flickering fear, that had come back into the deep blue eyes that for two months had looked into his with frank confidence.

He had made her acutely conscious of his displeasure. Only last night his lack of consideration and his unwonted irritability had made her wince several times during the evening.

After Saint Hubert had gone to his own tent, he had looked up to find her eyes fixed on him with an expression that, in his dangerous mood, had excited all the brutality of which he was capable, and had filled him with a desire to torture her.

The dumb reproach in her eyes had exasperated him, rousing the fiendish temper that had been hardly kept in check all the previous week.

Yet, when he held her helpless in his arms, quivering and shrinking from the embrace that was no caress, but merely the medium of his anger, and the reproach in her wavering eyes changed to mute entreaty, the pleasure he had anticipated in her fear had failed him.

The wild beating of her heart, the sobbing intake of her breath, and the knowledge of his power over her gave him no gratification.

He had flung her from him, cursing her savagely till she had fled into the other room with her hands over her ears to shut out the sound of his slow, deliberate voice.

And this morning he had left her without a sign of any kind, no word or gesture that might have effaced the memory of the previous night.

He had intended to go back to her before he finally rode away, but Saint Hubert's refusal to accompany him had killed the softer feelings that prompted him, and his rage had flamed up again.

And now? The longing to hold her in his arms, to kiss the tears from her eyes and the colour into her pale lips, was almost unbearable. He would give his life to keep even a shadow from her path, and she was in the hands of Ibraheim Omair!

The thought and all that it implied was torture, but no sign escaped him of the hell he was enduring.

Saint Hubert rose to his feet at last, and, leaving behind Henri and two Arabs, who were detailed to take the wounded man back to the camp, the swift gallop southward was resumed.

The distant howling of jackals came closer and

closer until, tipping one long rise and descending into a hollow that was long enough and wide enough to be fully lit by the moon, they came to the place where the ambush had been laid.

Instinctively Ahmed Ben Hassan knew that amongst the jostling heaps of corpses and dead horses lay the bodies of his own men. Perhaps amongst the still forms from which the jackals, whose hideous yelling they had heard, had slunk away, there might be one left with life enough to give some news.

One of his own men who would speak willingly, or one of Ibraheim Omair's who would be made to speak. His lips curled back from his white teeth in a grin of pure cruelty.

The silence that had prevailed amongst his men broke suddenly as they searched quickly among the dead.

The Sheik waited impassively, silent amidst the muttered imprecations and threats of vengeance of his followers as they laid beside him the six remains of what had been Diana's escort, slashed and mutilated almost beyond recognition.

But it was he who noticed that the last terrible figure stirred slightly as it was laid down, and it was into his face, grown suddenly strangely gentle, that the dying Arab looked with fast-filming eyes.

The man smiled, the happy smile of a child who has obtained an unexpected reward, and raised his hand painfully in salute, then pointed mutely to the south.

The Sheik caught his follower's nerveless fingers as they fell in his own strong grasp, and with a last effort the Arab drew his Chief's hand to his forehead and fell back dead.

Chapter
Eight

Slowly and painfully Diana struggled back to consciousness. The agony in her head was excruciating, and her limbs felt cramped and bruised. At first her thoughts were merged in physical suffering, but gradually the fog cleared from her brain and memory supervened hesitatingly. She remembered Gaston and the horror and resolution in his eyes, the convulsive working of his mouth as he faced her at the last moment.

Her own dread—not of the death that was imminent, but lest the mercy it offered should be snatched from her.

Then before the valet could effect his supreme devotion had come the hail of bullets, and he had fallen against her, the blood that poured from his wounds saturating her linen coat, and rolled over across her feet.

She remembered vaguely the wild figures hemming her in, but nothing more.

The desire to know where she was and what had happened made her forget her bruised body. She looked cautiously from under thick lashes, screened by the sleeve of her coat.

She was lying on a pile of cushions in one corner of a small tented apartment which was otherwise bare, except for the rug that covered the floor.

In the opposite corner of the tent an Arab woman crouched over a little brazier, and the smell of native coffee was heavy in the air.

Diana closed her eyes again with a shudder. The attempted devotion of Gaston had been useless. This must be the camp of the robber Sheik, Ibraheim Omair.

The little tent was intensely hot. The heat aggravated a burning thirst that was parching her throat. She got up on her feet slowly, and with infinite caution, to prevent any jar that might start again the throbbing in her head.

She crossed the tent to the side of the Arab woman.

"Give me some water," she said in French, but the woman shook her head without looking up.

Diana repeated the request in Arabic, one of the few sentences she knew without stumbling. This time the woman rose up hastily and held out a cup of the coffee she had been making.

Diana hated the sweet, thick stuff, but it would do until she could get the water she wanted, and she put out her hand to take the little cup. But her eyes met the other's, fixed on her, and something in their malignant stare made her pause.

A sudden suspicion shot through her mind. The coffee was drugged. What beyond the woman's expression made her think so she did not know, but she was sure of it. She put the cup aside impatiently.

"No. Not coffee. Water," she said firmly.

Before she realised what was happening, the woman thrust a strong arm round her and forced the cup to her lips. That confirmed Diana's suspicions, and rage lent her additional strength.

The woman was strong, but Diana was stronger, younger, and more active. She dashed the cup to the floor, spilling its contents.

She tore the clinging hands from her and sent the woman crashing onto the ground, rolling against the brazier, oversetting it, and scattering brass pots and cups over the rug.

The woman scrambled to her knees and beat out the glowing embers, uttering scream after scream in a shrill piercing voice. In answer to her cries, a curtain at the side of the tent, which Diana had not noticed, slid aside and a gigantic Nubian came in.

With outstretched hand shaking with rage, pointing at Diana, the woman burst into voluble abuse.

But Diana went a step forward, her head high, and looked him straight in the face.

"Fetch me water!" she said imperiously.

He pointed to the coffee that the woman had recommenced to make, her back now turned to them, but Diana stamped her foot.

"Water! Bring me water!" she said again.

With a wider grin the Negro made a gesture of acquiescence and went out, returning in a few moments with a water-skin.

The water was warm and slightly brackish, but she needed it too much to mind. In spite of being tepid it relieved the dry, suffocating feeling in her throat and refreshed her.

The Nubian went away again, leaving the woman still crouching over the brazier.

Diana walked back to the cushions and dropped down onto them gladly. The events of the last few moments had tried her more than she realised, her legs were shaking under her, and she was thankful to sit down.

But her courage had risen. The fact that she was physically stronger than the woman who had been put to guard her had a moral effect on her, restoring her confidence in herself.

Her position was an appalling one, but hope was strong within her. The fact that since she had regained consciousness she had seen only the woman and the Nubian seemed to argue that Ibraheim Omair must be absent from his camp.

If it could only be prolonged until Ahmed reached her. That the Sheik would come she knew, for her faith in him was unbounded. If he only came in time!

Hours had passed since the ambuscade had surprised them. It had been early afternoon then. Now the lighted lamp told her it was night. How late she did not know.

The Sheik would know her peril and he would come to her. Of that she had no doubt.

"He will come! He will come!"

She whispered it as if merely the sound of the words gave her courage. He would not let anything happen to her.

Every moment that Ibraheim Omair stayed away was so much gained; every moment Ahmed Ben Hassan would be coming nearer.

A sudden noise and men's voices in the adjoining room sent her to her feet. But the sharp, guttural voice predominating over the other voices killed the wild hope that had sprung up in her by its utter dissimilarity to the soft low tones for which she longed.

Ibraheim Omair had come first!

She stood rigid, one foot beating nervously

into the soft rug. She noticed irrelevantly at the moment that both her spurs and the empty holster had been removed whilst she was unconscious.

The voices in the next room continued, until Diana almost prayed that the moment she was waiting for would come; suspense was worse than the ordeal for which she was nerving herself.

It came at last. The curtain slid aside again, and the same huge Negro she had seen before entered. He came towards her and put out his hand as if to grasp her arm. But she stepped back with flashing eyes and a gesture that he obeyed.

Her heart was pounding, but she had herself under control. She walked slowly to the curtain and nodded to the Nubian to draw it aside, and slower still she passed into the other room.

It was only a little larger than the one she had left, and almost as bare, but her mind took in these things uncomprehendingly, for all her attention was focussed on the central figure in the room.

Ibraheim Omair, the robber Sheik, lolling his great bulk on a pile of cushions, and behind him, standing motionless as if formed of bronze, two other Negroes.

Diana paused for a moment framed in the entrance, then, with head thrown back, she moved across the thick rugs leisurely, and halted in front of the Chief, looking straight at him.

The hold she was exercising over herself was tremendous, her body was rigid with the effort, and her hands deep down in her pockets clenched till the nails bit into the palms. Every instinct was rebelling against the calm she forced upon herself.

She longed to scream and make a dash for the opening that she guessed was behind her, and to take her chance in the darkness outside.

But her only course lay in the bravado that alone kept her from collapse. She must convey the impression of fearlessness, though cold terror was knocking at her heart. Masked with indifference, her eyes were watching the robber Chief closely.

This was, indeed, the Arab of her imaginings. This gross figure lying among the tawdry cushions, his swollen, ferocious face seamed and lined with every mark of vice, his full, sensual lips parted and showing broken, blackened teeth.

His deep-set, bloodshot eyes had a look in them which took all her resolution to sustain, a look of such bestial evilness that the horror of it was terrifying.

His appearance was slovenly, his robes, originally rich, were stained and tumbled, the fat hands lying spread out on his knees were engrained with dirt, showing even against his dark skin.

His heavy face lit up with a gleam of malicious satisfaction as Diana came towards him, his loose mouth broadened in a wicked smile.

He leaned forward a little, weighing heavily on his hands, which were on his knees, his eyes roving slowly over her till they rested on her face again.

"So! The white woman of my brother Ahmed Ben Hassan," he said slowly, and with a sudden

167

snarling intonation as he uttered his enemy's name. "Ahmed Ben Hassan! May Allah burn his soul in hell!"

He spat contemptuously, and leaned back on the cushions with a grunt.

Diana kept her eyes fixed on him, and under their unwavering stare he seemed to be uneasy, his own inflamed eyes wandering ceaselessly over her, one hand fumbling at the curved hilt of a knife stuck in his belt.

At last he grew exasperated, hitching himself forward once more and beckoning her to come nearer to him. She hesitated, and as she paused uncertainly, there was a flutter of draperies behind her.

The Arab woman from the inner room, evading the Negro who stepped forward to stop her, flung herself at the feet of Ibraheim Omair, clinging to his knees with a low wailing cry.

In a flash Diana realised the meaning of the hatred that had gleamed in the woman's eyes earlier in the evening.

To her she was a rival, whose coming to share the favours of her lord had roused all the jealousy of the reigning favourite.

A wave of disgust mingled with the fear that was torturing Diana. Fighting against the terror that was growing on her, her lashes drooped and hid her eyes.

When she looked up again the woman was still crouched at the old Arab's feet, imploring and distraught.

Ibraheim Omair looked down on her, his lips drawn back from his blackened teeth in an evil grin.

Then he shook her off violently with a swift blow in the mouth, but the woman clung closer, with upturned, desperate face, a thin trickle of blood oozing from her lips.

With a hoarse growl that was like the dull roar of a savage beast, the robber Chief caught her by the throat, then slowly drew the long knife from the folds of his waist-cloth, and as slowly drove it home into the strangling woman's breast.

With savage callousness, before he released his hold of her, he wiped the stained knife carefully on her clothing and replaced it, and only then flung the dead body from him.

There was a momentary silence in the room, and Diana became conscious of a muffled, rhythmical beat near her, like the ticking of a great clock, and realised with dull wonder that it was her own heart beating.

She seemed turned to stone, petrified with the horror of the last few moments. Her eyes were glued to the still figure with the gaping wound in the breast, from which the blood was welling.

She felt physically sick for a moment, but very slowly she raised her head, and, meeting Ibraheim Omair's eyes fixed on her, she looked full at him across the dead woman's body and laughed!

It was that or shriek!

She must make no sign, she must not scream

or faint, she must keep her nerve until Ahmed came. Oh, dear God, send him quickly!

The laugh wavered hysterically, and she caught her lip between her teeth. She must do something to distract her attention from that awful still shape at her feet.

Then Ibraheim Omair leaned forward with a horrible leer and beckoned to Diana, patting the cushions beside him. Mastering the loathing that filled her, she sat down with all the unconcern she could assume.

The proximity of the man nauseated her. He reeked of sweat and grease and ill-kept horses.

She refused the coffee he offered her with a shake of her head, paying no attention to his growl of protest, not even understanding it, for he spoke in Arabic.

Then his fat hand closed about her wrist and he jerked her towards him.

"How many rifles did the Frenchman bring to that son of darkness?" he said harshly.

She turned her head, surprised at the question, and met his bloodshot eyes fixed on hers, half menacing, half admiring, and looked away again hastily.

"I do not know."

His fingers tightened on her wrist.

"How many men had Ahmed Ben Hassan in the camp in which he kept you?"

"I do not know."

"I do not know! I do not know!" he echoed with a sudden savage laugh. "You will know when I have done with you."

Question after question relating to the Sheik and his tribe followed in rapid succession, but to all of them Diana remained silent, with averted head and compressed lips.

"Later you will speak," he said significantly, and drank more coffee.

He kept his hold upon her, and presently, with a horrible loathing, she felt his hand passing over her arm, her neck, and down the soft curves of her slim young body, then with a muttered ejaculation he forced her to face him.

"What are you listening for? You think that Ahmed Ben Hassan will come? Little fool! He has forgotten you already. There are plenty more white women in Algiers and Oran that he can buy with his gold and his devil face." He laughed evilly.

"The loves of Ahmed Ben Hassan are as the stars in number. They come and go like the swift wind in the desert, a hot breath—and it's finished. He will not come, and if he does, he will not find you, for in an hour we shall be gone."

Diana writhed in his grasp. The hateful words in the guttural voice pronounced in vile French, the leering, vicious face with the light of admiration growing in the bloodshot eyes—all were a ghastly nightmare.

With a sudden desperate wrench she freed herself and fled across the tent—panic-stricken at last.

But in her blind rush she tripped, and with a swiftness that seemed incompatible with his unwieldiness Ibraheim Omair followed her and caught her in his arms.

Struggling, he carried her to the divan.

For a moment he paused, and instinctively Diana lay still, reserving her strength for the final struggle.

"One hour, my little gazelle, one hour—" he said hoarsely, and bent his face to hers.

With a cry Diana flung her head aside and strained away from him, fighting with the strength of madness. She fought like a boy with a swift thought of gratitude for Aubrey's training, and twisting she managed to slip through his grasp until her feet rested on the ground.

But his grip on her never relaxed; he dragged her back to him, ripping the thin shirt from her shoulders, baring her white breasts. Gasping, she struggled, until little by little his arms closed round her again.

She braced her hands against his chest, fending him from her till she felt that the muscles in her arms must crack, but the crushing force of his whole weight was bearing her steadily backwards, and downwards onto the soft cushions beside them.

His hot breath was on her face, the sickening reek of his clothes was in her nostrils. She felt her resistance growing weaker, her heart was labouring, beating with wild bounds that suffocated her.

The strength was going from her arms, only a moment more and her force would be exhausted.

Her brain was growing numbed, as it had been when the man who held her had murdered the woman before her eyes.

If he would only kill her now. Death would be easy compared with this!

The faint hope that still lingered was almost extinguished. Ahmed had not come!

In her agony the thought of him was a further torture. He would come, but he would come too late. He would never know now that she loved him. Oh, God! How she loved him! Ahmed! Ahmed!

With the soundless cry the last remnant of her strength went all at once, and she fell weakly against the Chief. He forced her to her knees, and, with his hand twined brutally in her curls, thrust her head back.

There was a mad light in his eyes and a foam on his lips as he dragged the knife from his waistbelt and laid the keen edge against her throat. She did not flinch, and after a moment he dropped it with a horrible laugh.

"No, afterwards," he said, and picked her up unresistingly. He flung her on the cushions and for one awful moment she felt his hands on her.

Then from outside came a sudden uproar and the sharp crack of rifle, and in a lull in the firing the Sheik's powerful voice:

"Diana! Diana!"

His voice and the knowledge of his nearness gave her new strength. She leapt up in spite of Ibraheim Omair's gripping hands.

"Ahmed!" she screamed.

Then the Chief's hand dashed against her mouth, but, frantic, she caught it in her teeth, biting it to the bone, and as he wrenched it away she shrieked again.

"Ahmed! Ahmed!"

It seemed impossible that her voice could be heard above the demoniacal noise outside the tent, and she could not call again, for with a snarl of rage the Chief caught her by the throat as he had caught the Arab woman.

Choking, stifling with the agony in her throat, her lungs seemed bursting, the blood was beating in her ears, and the room was darkening with the film that was creeping over her eyes.

The drumming in her ears grew louder and the tent was fading away into blackness. He was squeezing the life out of her and she heard his voice coming, as it were, from a great distance:

"You will not languish long in Hawiyat without your lover. I will send him quickly to you."

She was almost unconscious, but she heard the sneering voice break suddenly, and the deadly pressure on her throat relaxed as the Chief's hands rapidly transferred their grip to her aching shoulders, swinging her away from him and in front of him.

To lift her head was agony, and the effort brought back the black mist that had lessened with the slackening of Ibraheim Omair's fingers round her neck.

But it cleared again sufficiently for her to see, through a blurring haze, the outline of the tall figure that was facing her, standing by the ripped-back doorway.

There was a pause, a silence that contrasted oddly with the tumult outside, and Diana wondered numbly why the Sheik did nothing, why he did not use the revolver that was clenched in his hand.

Then slowly she understood that he dared not fire, that the Chief was holding her, a living shield, before him, sheltering himself behind the only thing that would deter Ahmed Ben Hassan's unerring shots.

Cautiously Ibraheim Omair moved backwards, still holding her before him, hoping to gain the inner room.

But in the shock of his enemy's sudden appearance he miscalculated the position of the divan and stumbled against it, losing his balance for only a moment, but long enough to give the man whose revolver covered him the chance he wanted.

With the cold ring of steel pressing against his forehead the robber Chief's hands dropped from Diana, and she slid weak and trembling onto the rug, clasping her pulsating throat, moaning with the effort that it was to breathe.

For a moment the two men looked into each other's eyes and the knowledge of death leapt into Ibraheim Omair's. With the fatalism of his creed he made no resistance as the Sheik's left hand reached out and fastened on his throat.

It would be quicker to shoot, but as Diana had suffered so should her torturer die. All the savagery in his nature rose uppermost.

Beside the pitiful, gasping little figure on the

rug at his feet there was the memory of six mutilated bodies, his faithful followers, men who had
grown to manhood with him.

The man who was responsible for their deaths
was in his power at last, but far beyond the feelings
inspired by the death of his followers was the desire
to kill, with his bare hands, the man who had tortured the woman he loved.

The knowledge of her peril, which had driven
him headlong through the night to her aid, the sight
of her helpless, agonised, in the robber Chief's
hands, had filled him with a madness that only the
fierce joy of killing would cure.

Before he could listen to the clamouring of
the new love in his heart, before he could gather up
into his arms the beloved little body, he had to de-
stroy the man whose murders were countless and
who had at last fallen into his hands.

The smile on his face deepened and his fingers
tightened slowly on their hold. But with the strangling clasp of Ahmed Ben Hassan's hands upon
him the love of life awoke again in Ibraheim Omair
and he struggled fiercely.

Crouched on the floor, Diana watched the two
big figures swaying in mortal embrace, with wide,
fearful eyes, her hands still holding her aching
throat. Ibraheim Omair wrestled for his life, conscious of his own strength, but conscious also of the
greater strength that was opposed to him.

The Sheik let go of the hold upon his throat
and with both arms locked about him manoeuvred
to get the position he required, back to the divan.

Then, with a wrestler's trick, he swept Ibraheim's feet from under him and sent his huge body sprawling onto the cushions, his knee on his enemy's chest, his hands on his throat.

With all his weight crushing into the Chief's breast, he choked him slowly to death, till the dying man's body ached and writhed in his last agony, and the blood burst from his nose and mouth, pouring over the hands that held him like a vise.

Diana's eyes never left the Sheik's face, she felt the old paralysing fear of him rushing over her, irresistibly drowning for the moment even the love she had for him.

She had seen him in cruel, even savage moods, but nothing that had ever approached the look on his face now.

The noise outside the tent was growing louder as the fighting rolled back in its direction, and once or twice a bullet ripped through the hangings.

One that came closer than the others made Diana turn her head and she saw what Ahmed Ben Hassan, absorbed in the fulfillment of his horrible task, had not even thought of—the three big Negroes and a dozen Arabs who had stolen in silently from the inner room.

For once the Sheik was careless and caught off his guard. Agony leapt into her eyes. She tried to warn him but no sound would come from her throbbing throat! She crawled nearer to him and touched him.

He dropped the dead Chief back into the tumbled cushions and looked up swiftly, and at the same moment Ibraheim Omair's men made a rush.

Without a word he thrust her behind the divan and turned to meet them. Before his revolver they gave way for a moment, but the burly Nubians behind swept the Arabs forward.

Three times he fired and one of the Negroes and two Arabs fell, but the rest hurled themselves on him, and Diana saw him surrounded.

His strength was abnormal, and for some minutes the struggling mass of men strained and heaved about him. Diana was on her feet, swaying giddily, powerless to help him, cold with dread.

Then above the clamour that was raging inside and out she heard Saint Hubert's voice shouting, and with a shriek that seemed to rip her tortured throat she called to him.

The Sheik, too, heard, and with a desperate effort for a moment won clear, but one of the Nubians was behind him.

As Saint Hubert and a crowd of the Sheik's own men poured in through the opening, he brought down a heavy club with crashing force on Ahmed Ben Hassan's head, and as he fell another drove a broad knife deep into his back.

Diana tried to get to him, faint and stumbling, flung here and there by the fighting, struggling men, until a strong hand caught her and drew her aside.

She strained against the detaining arm, but it was one of Ahmed's men. Mistily she saw Saint Hubert clear a way to his friend's side, and then she fainted, but only for a few moments.

Saint Hubert was still on his knees beside the Sheik when she opened her eyes, and the tent was quite quiet, filled with tribesmen waiting in stoical silence.

The camp of Ibraheim Omair had been wiped out, but Ahmed Ben Hassan's men looked only at the unconscious figure of their leader.

Saint Hubert glanced up hastily as Diana came to his side.

"You are all right?" he asked anxiously, but she did not answer. What did it matter about her?

"Is he going to die?" she said huskily, for speaking still hurt horribly.

"I don't know—but we must get away from here. I need more appliances than I have with me, and we are too few to stay and risk a possible attack if there are more of Ibraheim Omair's men in the neighbourhood."

Diana looked down on the wounded man fearfully.

"But the ride—the jolting," she gasped.

"It has to be risked," replied Saint Hubert abruptly.

* * *

Of the long, terrible journey back to Ahmed Ban Hassan's camp Diana never remembered very much. From time to time Saint Hubert spoke to her, and the quiet courage of his voice steadied her breaking nerves.

As they passed the scene of the ambuscade he told her of Gaston. It was there that the first band of waiting men had met them, warned already of their coming by a couple of Arabs whom the *Vicomte* had sent on in advance with the news.

The dawn was breaking when they reached the camp. Diana had a glimpse of rows of unusually silent men grouped beside the tent, but all her mind was concentrated on the long, limp figure that was being carefully lifted down from the sweating horse.

They carried him into the tent and laid him on the divan, beside which Henri had already put out all the implements that his master would need.

While Saint Hubert, with difficulty, cleared the tent, Diana stood beside the divan and looked at the Sheik.

He was soaked in blood that had burst through the temporary bandages, and his whole body bore evidence of the terrible struggle that had gone before the blow that had felled him.

One blood-covered hand hung down, almost touching the rug. Diana lifted it in her own, and the touch of the nerveless fingers sent a sob into her throat. She caught her lip between her teeth to stop it from trembling as she laid his hand down on the cushions.

Saint Hubert came in, rolling up his shirtsleeves significantly.

"Diana, you have been through enough," he said gently. "Go and rest while I do what I can for Ahmed. I will come and tell you as soon as I am finished."

She looked up fiercely.

"It's no good telling me to go away, because

I won't. I must help you. I can help you. I shall go mad if you don't let me do something. See! My hands are quite steady."

She held them out as she spoke, and Saint Hubert gave in without opposition.

All through the horrible time that followed she did not falter. Her face was deadly pale, and dark lines showed below her eyes, but her hands did not shake, and her voice was low and even.

She suffered horribly. The terrible wound that the Nubian's knife had made was like a wound in her own heart. She winced as if the hurt had been her own when Saint Hubert's gentle, dexterous fingers touched the Sheik's bruised head.

When it was over and Raoul had turned aside to wash his hands she slipped onto her knees beside him. Would he live? She looked at him with anguished eyes.

Only a few hours before, he had come to her in all the magnificence of his strength. She looked at the long limbs lying now so still, so terribly, suggestively still, and her lips trembled again, but her pain-filled eyes were dry.

She could not cry, only her throat ached and throbbed perpetually. She leaned over him, whispering his name, and a sudden hunger came to her to touch him, to convince herself that he was not dead.

"Ahmed, oh, my dear!" she whispered unsteadily, and kissed him with lips that quivered against the stillness of his.

Then for a moment she dropped her bright

head beside the bandaged one on the pillow, but when the *Vicomte* came back she was kneeling where he had left her, her hands clasped over one of the Sheik's and her face hidden against the cushions.

Saint Hubert put his hand on her shoulder.

"Diana, you are torturing yourself unnecessarily. We cannot know for some time how it will go with him. Try to get some sleep for a few hours. You can do no good by staying here. Henri and I will watch. I will call you if there is any change, my word of honour."

She shook her head without looking up.

"I can't go. I couldn't sleep."

Saint Hubert did not press it.

"Very well," he said quietly, "but if you are going to stay you must take off your riding boots and put on something more comfortable than those clothes."

She realised the sense of what he was saying, and obeyed him without a word.

When she came back Henri was pouring coffee, and Saint Hubert turned to her with a cup in his outstretched hand.

"Please take it. It will do you good," he said, with a little smile that was not reflected in his anxious eyes.

She took it, unheeding, and, swallowing it hastily, went to the side of the divan again. She slid down onto the rug where she had knelt before.

The Sheik was lying as she had left him. For a few moments she looked at him, then drowsily her eyes closed and her head fell forward on the cushions, and with a half-sad smile of satisfaction Saint Hubert gathered her up into his arms.

He carried her into the bedroom, hesitating beside the couch before he put her down, very gently drawing the thin coverlet over her, and went back slowly to the other room.

He sent Henri away and sat down beside the divan to watch with a feeling of weariness that was not bodily. He had need for all his calm, and he gripped himself resolutely.

For a time Ahmed Ben Hassan lay motionless, and then, as the day crept on, and the early rays of the warm sun filled the tent, he moved uneasily, and began to mutter feverishly in confused Arabic and French.

At first the words that came were almost unintelligible, pouring out with rapid indistinctness, then by degrees his voice slowed, and hesitating, interrupted sentences came clearly from his lips.

And beside him, with his face buried in his hands, Raoul de Saint Hubert thanked God fervently that he had saved Diana the added torture of listening to the revelations of the past four months.

The first words were in Arabic, then the slow, soft voice lapsed into French, pure as the *Vicomte*'s own.

"Two hours south of the oasis with the three broken palm trees by the well . . . Lie still, you little fool, it is useless to struggle. You cannot get away, I shall not let you go. . . .

"Why have I brought you here? You ask me

why? *Mon Dieu!* Are you not woman enough to know? No! I will not spare you. Give me what I want willingly and I will be kind to you, but fight me, and by Allah! you shall pay the cost! . . .

"I know you hate me, you have told me so already. Shall I make you love me? . . . Still disobedient? When will you learn that I am master? . . . I have not tired of you yet, you lovely little wild thing, *garçon manqué.* . . .

"You say she is cowed; I say she is content—content to give me everything I ask of her. . . . For four months she has fought me.

"Why does it give me no pleasure to have broken her at last? Why do I want her still?

"She is English and I have made her pay for my hatred of her cursed race. I have tortured her to keep my vow, and still I want her. . . .

"Diana, Diana, how beautiful you are! . . .

"Allah! how long the day has been. . . . Has it been long to her? Will she smile or tremble when I come? . . . Where is Diana? . . .

"Diana, Diana, how could I know how much you meant to me? How could I know that I should love you? . . . Diana, Diana, my sunshine. The tent is cold and dark without you. . . .

"Ibraheim Omair! That devil and Diana!

"Oh, Allah! Grant me time to get to her. . . . How the jackals are howling! . . . See, Raoul, there are the tents. . . . Diana, where are you? . . . *Grand Dieu!* He has been torturing her! . . .

"You knew that I would come, *ma bien aimée,* only a few moments while I kill him, then I can hold you in my arms. *Dieu!* If you knew how much I loved you . . . Diana, Diana, it is all black. I cannot see you, Diana, Diana. . . ."

Hour after hour with weary hopelessness the tired voice went on—

"Diana, Diana . . ."

Chapter
Nine

It was evening when Diana opened drowsy and heavy eyes, a bitter taste in her mouth from the effects of the drug that Saint Hubert had given her.

The tiny chime of her clock sounded seven times, and with a rush of recollection she leapt up.

More than twelve hours had passed since she had knelt beside him after drinking the coffee that Raoul had given her.

She guessed what he had done and tried to be grateful, but the thought of what might have happened during the twelve hours she had lain like a log was horrible.

She dressed with feverish haste and went into the outer room; the *Vicomte* brought a chair for her.

"Sit down," he said almost gruffly. "You look like a ghost."

She looked up at him reproachfully.

"You drugged that coffee, Raoul. If he had died today while I was asleep I don't think I could ever have forgiven you."

"My dear child," he said gravely, "you don't know how near you were to collapse. If I had not made you sleep I should have had three patients on my hands instead of two."

"I am very ungrateful," she murmured, with a tremulous little smile.

Saint Hubert brought a chair for himself and dropped into it wearily. He looked across the divan at Diana, and the change that the last few hours had made in her struck him painfully.

She sighed, and Saint Hubert rose and bent over the Sheik with his fingers on his wrist. As he laid the nerveless hand down again she leaned nearer and covered it with her own.

"His hand is so big for an Arab's," she said

softly, like a thought spoken aloud unconsciously.

"He is not an Arab," replied Saint Hubert with sudden, impatient vehemence. "He is English."

Diana looked up at him swiftly with bewilderment in her startled eyes.

"I don't understand," she faltered. "He hates the English."

"Quand-même, he is the son of one of your English peers. His mother was Spanish. Has he never told you anything about himself?"

She shook her head.

"Sometimes I have wondered—" she said reflectively. "He seemed different from the others, and there has been so much that I could not understand. But then again there were times when he seemed pure Arab."

"You ought to know," said Saint Hubert. "Yes! It will explain so many things. I will take the responsibility. His father is the Earl of Glencaryll."

"But I know him," said Diana wonderingly. "He was a friend of my father."

"I had better tell you the whole story," said Raoul, dropping back into his chair.

"Thirty-six years ago my father, who was as great a wanderer as I am, was staying here in the desert with his friend the Sheik Ahmed Ben Hassan.

"The Sheik was a wonderful man, very enlightened, with strong European tendencies. He was unmarried, and the women of his own race seemed to have no attraction for him.

"My father had come for a stay of some

months. My mother had recently died and he wanted to get away from everything that reminded him of her.

"One evening, shortly after his arrival at the camp, a party of the Sheik's men who had been absent for some days in the north on the Chief's affairs arrived, bringing with them a woman whom they had found wandering in the desert.

"How she had got there, or from what direction she had come, they did not know. She could give no account of herself, as, owing to the effects of the sun or other causes, she was temporarily out of her mind.

"She was taken to the tent of one of the headmen, whose wife looked after her. For some days it was doubtful whether she would recover, and her condition was aggravated by the fact that she was shortly to become a mother.

"She did regain her senses after a time, but nothing could make her say anything about herself.

"She was quite young. From her accent my father decided that she was Spanish, but she would admit nothing, not even her nationality. In due course of time the child was born, a boy."

Saint Hubert paused a moment and nodded towards the Sheik.

"Even after the child's birth she refused to give any account of herself. She nearly died when the baby was born, and she never recovered her strength.

"The Sheik, who had never looked twice at a

woman before in his life, became passionately attached to her. My father says that he has never seen a man so madly in love as Ahmed Ben Hassan was with the strange white girl.

"He repeatedly implored her to marry him, but she would not consent.

"Her refusal made no difference with the Sheik. His devotion was wonderful.

"When she died my father was again visiting the camp. She knew that she was dying, and a few days before the end she told them her pitiful little history.

"She was the only daughter of one of the oldest noble houses in Spain, and she had been married when she was seventeen to Lord Glencaryll. He had a terrible temper that was very easily roused, and when under the influence of drink behaved more like a devil than a man.

"He made no allowance for her youth and inexperience, and her life was one long torture. And yet in spite of it all she loved him.

"It seems that Lord Glencaryll had taken her to Algiers and had wished to make a trip into the desert. He had been drinking heavily, and she did not dare to upset his plans by refusing to go with him or even by telling him how soon her child was going to be born.

"One night something happened—what she would not say, but my father says he has never seen such a look of terror on any woman's face as she hurried over that part of her story.

"Whatever it was, she waited until the camp was asleep and then slipped out into the desert, mad with fear, with no thought beyond a blind instinct of flight that drove her panic-stricken to face any danger rather than remain.

"She wrote a letter for her husband which she gave into my father's keeping, together with her wedding ring, which had an inscription inside of it, and a miniature of Glencaryll which she had worn always hidden away from sight.

"She was very contrite with the Sheik, begging his forgiveness for the sorrow she had caused him and for keeping from his knowledge the fact that she was not free.

"She loved her husband loyally to the end, but the last few days that she lived the Sheik's devotion seemed to wake an answering tenderness in her heart. She was happiest when he was with her, and she died in his arms with his kisses on her lips.

"She left her boy in his keeping, and Ahmed Ben Hassan adopted him formally and made him his heir, giving him his own name.

"All the passionate love that the Sheik had for the mother was transferred to the son. He idolised him, and the boy grew up believing that Ahmed Ben Hassan was his own father.

"When he was fifteen my father induced the Sheik to send him to Paris to be educated. He loathed the restrictions that had to be put upon him and he hated the restraint of town life.

"The only thing that he studied seriously was

veterinary surgery, which he knew would be useful to him with his own horses, and in which his tutor was level-headed enough to encourage him.

"Then at the end of the two years he came back to us for another year. He was nineteen then, and when he was twenty-one my father had the unpleasant task of carrying out Lady Glencaryll's dying wishes.

"He wrote to Lord Glencaryll asking him to come to Paris on business connected with his late wife, and, during the course of a very painful interview, put all the facts before him.

"With the letter that the poor girl had written to her husband, with the wedding ring and the locket, together with the sketch that my father had made of her, the proofs of the genuineness of the whole affair were conclusive.

"Glencaryll broke down completely. He had ardently desired an heir, and, thinking himself childless, the fact that his title and his old name, of which he was very proud, would die with him had been a great grief.

"His happiness in the knowledge of Ahmed's existence was pathetic, and he was consumed with impatience for his son's arrival.

"Nothing had been said to Ahmed in case Lord Glencaryll should prove difficult to convince, but his ready acceptance of the affair and his eagerness to see his son made further delay unnecessary, and my father sent for Ahmed.

"The old Sheik let him go in ignorance of what

was coming. He had always dreaded the time when his adopted son would have to be told of his real parentage, fearful of losing him, jealous of sharing his affection, and resenting anybody's claim to him over his own.

"He sent Ahmed to Paris with no explanation, and left to my father the task of breaking the news to him.

"He never said a word the whole time my father was speaking, and when he finished he stood quite still for a few moments, his face almost grey under the deep tan, his eyes fixed passionately on my father's—and then his fiendish temper broke out suddenly.

"It was a terrible scene. He cursed his father in a steady stream of mingled Arabic and French blasphemy that made one's blood run cold. He cursed all English people impartially. He cursed my father because he had dared to send him to England.

"He cursed me because I had been a party to the affair.

"The only person whom he spared was the Sheik, who after all was as much implicated as we were, but he never once mentioned him.

"He refused to see his father, refused to recognise that he was his father, and he left the house that afternoon and Paris that night, going straight back to the desert, taking with him Gaston, who had arranged sometime before to enter his service.

"From the day he learned the truth about himself for two years we saw nothing of him. Then the old Sheik asked us to visit him. We went with some misgivings as to what Ahmed's reception of us would be, but he met us as if nothing had happened. He ignored the whole episode and has never referred to it.

"The Sheik warned us that Ahmed had told him that any reference to it would mean the breaking off of all relations with us. But Ahmed himself had changed indescribably.

"All the lovable qualities that had made him so popular in Paris were gone, and he had become the cruel, merciless man he has been ever since. The only love left in him was given to his adopted father, whom he worshipped."

Saint Hubert broke off and looked anxiously at Diana. She was sitting with her hand still clasped over the Sheik's, and the *Vicomte* went on speaking:

"It is so easy to judge, so difficult to understand another person's temptations. Ahmed's position has always been a curious one. He has had unique temptations with always the means of gratifying them."

There was a longer pause, but Diana did not move or speak.

Saint Hubert went on:

"Five years ago the old Sheik died. Ahmed's devotion during his illness was wonderful. He never left him, and since he succeeded to the leadership of the tribe he has lived continuously amongst his people, carrying on the traditions handed down to him by his predecessor and devoting his life to the tribe."

Saint Hubert stopped abruptly. Diana did not speak, and he felt that she wanted to be alone.

She watched him go, then slipped to her knees beside the couch.

She could not think of Ahmed as an Englishman. He was and always would be an Arab of the wilderness. If he lived! He *must* live!

She loved him well enough to sacrifice anything for him. If he only lived she could bear even to be put out of his life.

He was so young, so strong, so made to live. He was essential to his people.

If she could only die for him. If God would but listen to her now. If He would but accept her life in exchange for his. If—! If—!

She drew a long sobbing breath.

"Ahmed, *mon bel Arabe,*" she murmured yearningly.

She rose to her feet. She was afraid of breaking down, so she went to see Saint Hubert.

"You must be very tired, Raoul," she said.

"I must not think of that yet," he replied. "Later on, perhaps, I can rest a little. Henri can watch; he is almost as good a doctor as I am, the incomparable Henri!"

They stood in silence for a while, watching the shifting groups of tribesmen.

"The men are restless," Raoul said. "Their devotion is very strong. Ahmed is a god to them."

She turned back into the tent with Saint Hubert. They halted by the couch and stood for a long time in silence.

Then Diana slowly raised her head and looked up into Raoul's face, and he read the agonised question in her eyes.

"I don't know," he said gently. "All things are with Allah."

Chapter
Ten

It was three months since the night that Saint Hubert had almost given up hope of being able to save the Sheik's life—a night that had been followed by days of suspense that had reduced Diana to a weary-eyed shadow of her former vigorous self.

But thanks to his great strength and splendid constitution the Sheik had rallied and after the first few weeks convalescence had been rapid.

Only once had he referred to the raid. As Diana bent over him to do some small office his fingers closed feebly round her wrist and his eyes looked into hers for the first time since the night when she had fled from his curses.

"Was it—in time?" he whispered slowly.

As she nodded with crimson cheeks and lowered eyes, he turned his head away without another word, but a shudder that he was too weak to control shook him.

The camp soon settled down into normal conditions, but with the Sheik's complete recovery his attitude towards Diana had reverted to the cold reserve that had chilled her before.

He had avoided her as much as had been possible, and the continual presence of Saint Hubert had been a barrier between them.

Though he included her in the general conversation at meals, he rarely spoke to her directly, and often she found him looking at her with his fierce eyes filled with an expression that baffled her.

He had slept in the outer room since his illness, and tossing feverishly on the soft cushions of the big empty bed in which she lay alone Diana had suffered the greatest humiliation she had yet experienced.

He had never loved her, but now he did not

even want her. She was useless to him. She was less than nothing to him. He had no need of her.

In the daytime, too, she had been much alone, for as soon as the Sheik was strong enough to sit in the saddle he and Raoul had ridden far afield every day.

At last the *Vicomte* had announced that his visit could be protracted no longer and that he must resume his journey to Morocco.

His decision once made, he had speeded every means of getting away. To Diana his going meant the hastening of a crisis that could not be put off much longer.

This morning he and Ahmed Ben Hassan had ridden away at daybreak.

She had ridden with Gaston, and hurried over her solitary dinner, and since then she had been waiting for the Sheik to come back. In what mood would he come?

Tonight her nerves were on edge. She was restless and excited, and her thoughts were chaos.

She was alone again at his mercy. What would his attitude be? Her hands clenched her knees. She longed for him passionately, and at the same time she was afraid.

She had never been nervous before, but tonight her imagination ran riot. Was the love that had changed her so completely also making her a coward?

Ahmed Ben Hassan had tamed her as he tamed the magnificent horses that he rode. He had been brutal and merciless, using no half measures, forcing her to obedience by sheer strength of will and compelling a complete submission.

She thought of how she had feared and hated him with passionate intensity, until the hatred had been swamped by love as passionate and as intense.

She crossed to the doorway and pulled aside the flap, and a small, white-clad figure rose up before her.

"Is that you, Gaston?" she asked involuntarily, though she knew that the question was unnecessary, for he always slept across the entrance to the tent when the Sheik was away.

"À votre service, Madame."

For a few minutes she did not speak, and Gaston stood silent beside her. She might have remembered that he was there. He never stirred far beyond the sound of her voice whenever she was alone in the camp. He was always waiting, unobtrusive, quick to carry out her requests, even to anticipate them.

"Madame is tired?" Gaston's voice murmured at her ear.

"It is so hot. The tent was stifling," she replied evasively.

Gaston's devotion was of a kind that sought practical demonstration.

"Madame veut du café?" he suggested tentatively.

"No, it is too late."

"In one little moment I will bring it," Gaston urged persuasively.

She shook her head.

"No, Gaston. It makes me nervous. *Monseigneur* is late."

"He will come," replied Gaston confidently. "Kopec is restless, he is always so when *Monseigneur* is coming."

She looked down for a moment thoughtfully at the dim shape of the hound lying at the man's feet; all the time her ears were strained to catch the earliest sound of the Sheik's arrival.

At last it came. Only a suggestion at first—a wave of thought caught by her waiting brain, an instinctive intuition, and she started up tense with expectancy, her lips parted, her eyes wide, hardly breathing, listening intently.

And when he came it was with unexpected suddenness, for, in the darkness, the little bank of horsemen were invisible until they were right on the camp, and the horses' hoofs made no sound.

One of the horses whinnied, and then in the ensuing silence she heard him come into the tent. Her heart raced suffocatingly.

Her face was quite white, even her lips were colourless, and her eyes were fixed on the curtain which divided the two rooms.

He was pacing up and down as he had paced on the night when Gaston's fate was hanging in the balance, as he always paced when he was deliberating anything, and the scent of his cigarette filled her room.

Once he paused near the communicating curtain and her heart gave a wild leap, but after a moment he moved away. He stopped again at the far end of the tent, and she knew from the faint metallic click that he was loading his revolver.

She gave a quick, impatient sigh, and the tender light in her eyes deepened into an anxiety that was half maternal.

At last she heard the divan creak under his weight, but not until Gaston came back, bringing his supper.

Why was Ahmed drinking French coffee, which he always complained kept him awake? Surely tonight he had need of sleep. It was the hardest day he had had since his illness.

Diana was starving for the touch of his hands, suffering horribly. She slid down onto her knees, burying her face in the couch.

"Oh, God! Give me his love!" she kept whispering in agonised entreaty.

The recollection of the night, months before, when in the same posture she had prayed that God's curse might fall on him, sent a shudder through her.

"I didn't mean it," she moaned. "Oh, dear God! I didn't mean it. I didn't know . . . Take it back. I didn't mean it."

She choked down the sobs that rose, pressing her face closer into the silken coverings.

There was silence in the next room except for the striking of a match that came with monotonous regularity. As always, the peculiar scent of his tobacco drifted in through the heavy curtains, forcing a hundred recollections with the association of its perfume.

Why didn't he come to her? Did he know how he was torturing her? Was he so utterly indifferent that he did not care what she suffered? Did he even think of her?

The fear of the future rushed on her again with overwhelming force. The uncertainty was killing her. She raised her head and looked at the travelling clock beside the reading-lamp. It was an hour since Gaston had left him. Another hour of waiting would drive her mad.

She must know what he was going to do. She could bear anything but this suspense. She had reached the limit of her endurance.

She struggled to her feet, drawing the thin wrap closer round her. But even then she stood irresolute, dreading the fulfilling of her fears. Her eyes were fixed on the clock, watching the hands drag slowly round the dial. A quarter of an hour crept past.

It seemed the quarter of a lifetime. No sound of any kind came now from the other room. The silence was driving her frantic. She was desperate; she must know, nothing could be worse than the agony she was enduring.

She set her teeth and, crossing the room, slipped noiselessly between the curtains. Then she shrank back suddenly with her hands over her mouth. He was leaning forward on the divan, his elbows on his knees, his face hidden in his hands.

It was as a stranger that he had come back to her, divested of the flowing robes that had seemed essentially a part of him; an unfamiliar figure in silk shirt, riding breeches and high brown boots, still dust-covered from the long ride.

A thin tweed coat lay in a heap on the carpet —he must have flung it off after Gaston went, for the valet, with his innate tidiness, would never have left it lying on the floor.

She looked at him hungrily, her eyes ranging slowly over the long length of him and lingering on his bent head. She was shaking with a sudden new shyness, but love gave her courage and she went to him, her bare feet noiseless on the rugs.

"Ahmed!" she whispered.

He lifted his head slowly, and looked at her, and the sight of his face sent her onto her knees beside him, her hands clutching the breast of his soft shirt.

"Ahmed! What is it? . . . You are hurt—your wound—?" she cried, her voice sharp with anxiety.

He caught her groping hands, and rising, pulled her gently to her feet, his fingers clenched round hers, looking down at her strangely.

Then he turned from her without a word, and wrenching open the flap of the tent, flung it back and stood in the open doorway, staring out into the night.

"What is it?" she whispered again breathlessly.

"We start for Oran tomorrow," he replied.

His voice sounded dull and curiously strange, and with a little start Diana realised that he was speaking in English. Her eyes closed and she swayed dizzily.

"You are sending me away?" she gasped slowly.

There was a pause before he answered.

"Yes."

"Why?"

He did not answer and the colour flamed suddenly into her face. She went closer to him, her breast heaving, trying to speak, but her throat was parched and her lips were shaking so that no words would come.

"It is because you are tired of me?" she muttered at last hoarsely. "As you told me you would tire, as you tired of those other women?"

Her voice died away with an accent of horror in it. He did not answer but he winced, and his hands, which were hanging at his sides, clenched slowly.

He spoke at length in the same level, toneless voice.

"I will take you to the first desert station outside of Oran, where you can join the train. For your own sake I must not be seen with you in Oran, as I am known there.

"If you should by any chance be recognised or your identity should leak out, you can say that for reasons of your own you extended your trip, that your messages miscarried, anything that occurs to you.

"But it is not at all likely to happen. There are many travellers passing through Oran. Gaston can do all business and make all arrangements for you. He will take you to Marseilles, and if you need him he will go with you to Paris, Cherbourg, or London—whichever you wish.

"When you do not need him any longer, he will come back to me. I—I will not trouble you anymore. You need never be afraid that I will come into your life again.

"You can forget these months in the desert and the uncivilised Arab who crossed your path. To keep out of your way is the only amends I can make."

She flung up her head. Quick, suspicious jealousy and love and pride contending nearly choked her.

"Why don't you speak the truth?" she cried wildly. "Why don't you say what you really mean? —that you have no further use for me, that it amused you to take me and torture me to satisfy your whim, but the whim is passed.

"You are tired of me and so you get rid of me with all precautions. Do you think the truth can hurt me? Nothing that you can do can hurt me now.

"You made me the vile thing I am for your pleasure, and now for your pleasure you throw me on one side. . . .

"How many times a year does Gaston take your discarded mistresses back to France?"

Her voice broke into a terrible laugh.

He swung round swiftly and flung his arms about her, crushing her to him savagely, forgetting his strength, his eyes blazing.

"God! Do you think it is easy to let you go,

that you are taunting me like this? Do you think I haven't suffered, that I'm not suffering now?

"Don't you know that it is tearing my heart out by the roots to send you away?

"My life will be hell without you. Do you think I haven't realised what an infinitely damned brute I've been? I didn't love you when I took you, I only wanted you to satisfy the beast in me.

"And I was glad that you were English so that I could make you suffer as an Englishman made my mother suffer, I so loathed the whole race. I have been mad all my life, I think—up till now.

"I thought I didn't care until the night I heard that Ibraheim Omair had got you, and then I knew that if anything happened to you the light of my life was out, and that I would only wait to kill Ibraheim before I killed myself."

His arms were like a vise hurting her, but they felt like heaven, and she clung to him speechless, her heart throbbing wildly. He looked down long and deeply into her eyes, and the light in his—the light that she had longed for—made her tremble.

His brown head bent lower and lower, and his lips had almost touched her when he drew back, and the love in his eyes faded into misery.

"I mustn't kiss you," he said huskily, as he put her from him gently. "I don't think I should have the courage to let you go if I did. I didn't mean to touch you."

He turned from her with a little gesture of weariness.

"I don't want to go," she whispered faintly.

He paused by the writing-table and took up the revolver he had loaded earlier, breaking it absently, spinning the magazine between his finger and thumb, and replaced it before answering.

"You don't understand. There is no other way," he said dully.

"If you really loved me you would not let me go," she cried with a miserable sob.

"*If* I loved you?" he echoed, with a hard laugh. "*If* I loved you! It is because I love you so much that I am able to do it. If I loved you a little *less* I would let you stay and take your chance."

She flung out her hands appealingly.

"I want to stay, Ahmed. I love you!" she panted, desperate—for she knew his obstinate determination, and she saw her chance of happiness slipping away.

He did not move or look at her, and his brows drew together in the dreaded heavy frown.

"You don't know what you are saying. You don't know what it would mean," he replied in a voice from which he had forced all expression.

"If you married me you would have to live always here in the desert. I cannot leave my people, and I am—too much of an Arab to let you go alone. It would be no life for you.

"You think you love me now, though God knows how you can alter what I have done to you, but a time would come when you would find that your love for me did not compensate for your life here.

"And marriage with me is unthinkable. You know what I am and what I have been. I am not fit to live with, not fit to be near, any decent woman.

"My devilish temper—it has not spared you in the past, and it might not spare you in the future.

"Do you think that I could bear to see you year after year growing to hate me more? You think that I am cruel now, but I am thinking what is best for you afterwards.

"Someday you will think of me a little kindly because I had the strength to let you go. You are so young, your life is only just beginning. Forget the past and live only for the future."

He drew in his breath, and went on.

"You must go back to your own country, to your own people, to your own life, in which I have no place or part, and soon all this will seem only like an ugly dream."

She shuddered convulsively.

"Ahmed! I *can't* go!" she wailed.

He looked up sharply, his face livid, and tore her hands from her face.

"Good God! You don't mean—I haven't— you aren't—" He gasped hoarsely, looking down at her with a great fear in his eyes.

She guessed what he meant and the colour rushed into her face. The temptation to lie to him and let the consequences rest with the future was almost more than she could resist.

One little word and she would be in his arms . . . but afterwards—? It was the fear of the afterwards that kept her silent. The colour slowly drained from her face and she shook her head mutely.

He let go of her wrists with a quick sigh of relief and wiped the perspiration from his face. Then he laid his hand on her shoulder and pushed her gently towards the inner room.

For a moment she resisted, her wide, desperate eyes searching his, but he would not meet her look, and his mouth was set in the hard, straight line she knew so well, and with a cry she flung herself on his breast, her face hidden against him, her hands clinging round his neck.

"Ahmed! Ahmed! You are killing me. I cannot live without you. I love you and I want you—only you. I am not afraid of the loneliness of the desert, it is the loneliness of the world outside the shelter of your arms of which I am afraid!

"I never lived until you taught me what life was, here in the desert. I can't go back to the old life, Ahmed. Have pity on me. Don't shut me out from my only chance of happiness, don't send me away.

"I know you love me—I know! I know! And because I know, I am not ashamed to beg you to be merciful. I haven't any shame or pride left. Ahmed! Speak to me! I can't bear your silence. . . . Oh! You are cruel, cruel!"

"I have never been anything else," he said bitterly, "but I am willing that you should think me a brute now rather than that you should live to curse the day you ever saw me."

He paused and continued:

"It is very late. We must start early. Go and lie down."

It was an order in spite of the gentleness of his voice.

She shrank back, trembling, with stricken face and eyes filled with a great despair. She knew him and she knew it was the end. Nothing would break his resolution.

She looked at him with quivering lips through a mist of tears, looked at him with a desperate fixedness that sought to memorise indelibly his beloved image in her heart.

The dear head so proudly poised on the broad shoulders, the long, strong limbs, the slender, graceful body. He was all good to look upon.

A rush of tears blinded her and she stepped back uncertainly and stumbled against the little writing-table.

She caught at it behind her to steady herself, and her fingers touched the revolver he had laid down.

The contact of the cold metal sent a chill that seemed to strike her heart. She stood rigid, with startled eyes fixed on the motionless figure in the doorway—one hand gripping the weapon tightly and the other clutching the silken wrap across her breast.

Her mind raced forward feverishly, there were only a few hours left before the morning, before the bitter moment when she must leave behind her forever the surroundings that had become so dear, that had been her home as the castle in England had never been.

What was life without him? Nothing and less than nothing. She could never give herself to another man. She was necessary to no one. Aubrey had no need of her.

Slowly she lifted the weapon clear of the table with steady fingers and brought her hand stealthily from behind her. She looked at it for a moment dispassionately.

She was not afraid. She was conscious only of an overwhelming weariness, a longing for rest that should still the gnawing pain in her breast and the throbbing in her head. . . .

She lifted the revolver to her temple resolutely.

There had been no sound to betray what was passing behind him, but the extra sense, the consciousness of imminent danger that was strong in the desert-bred man, sprang into active force within the Sheik.

He turned like a flash and leapt across the space that separated them, catching her hand as she pressed the trigger, and the bullet sped harmlessly an inch above her head.

With his face gone suddenly ghastly he wrenched the weapon from her and flung it far into the night.

For a moment they stared into each other's eyes in silence, then, with a moan, she slipped from his grasp and fell at his feet in an agony of terrible weeping.

With a low exclamation he stooped and swept

her up into his arms, holding her slender, shaking figure with tender strength, pressing her head against him, his cheek on her red-gold curls.

"My God! Child, don't cry so. I can bear anything but that," he cried brokenly.

But the terrible sobs went on, and fearfully he caught her closer, straining her to him convulsively, raining kisses on her shining hair.

"Diana, Diana," he whispered imploringly, falling back into the soft French that seemed so much more natural.

"My darling one, my little love. Do not cry, I beg you. I love you! I adore you! You are mine, all mine."

She seemed only half conscious, unable to check the emotion that, unloosed, overwhelmed her. She lay inert against him, racked with the long, shuddering sobs that shook her.

His firm mouth quivered as he looked down at his work. Gathering her up to his heart, he carried her to the divan, and the weight of her soft slim body sent the blood racing madly through his veins.

He laid her down, and dropped to his knees beside her, his arms wrapped round her, whispering words of passionate love.

Gradually the terrible shuddering passed and the gasping sobs died away, and she lay still, so still and white that he was afraid. He tried to rise to fetch some restorative, but at the first movement she clung to him, pressing closer to him.

"I don't want anything but you," she murmured almost inaudibly.

His arm tightened round her and he turned her face up to his. Her eyes were closed and the wet lashes lay black against her pale cheek. His lips touched them pitifully.

"Diana, will you never look at me again?"

His voice was almost humble.

Her eyes quivered a moment and then opened slowly, looking up into his with a still-lingering fear in them.

"You won't send me away?" she whispered pleadingly, like a terrified child.

A hard sob broke from him and he kissed her trembling lips fiercely.

"Never!" he said sternly. "I will never let you go now. My God! If you knew how I wanted you. If you knew what it cost me to send you away. Pray God I keep you happy. You know the worst of me, poor child—you will have a devil for a husband."

The colour stole back slowly into her face and a little tremulous smile curved her lips. She slid her arm up and round his neck, drawing his head down.

"I am not afraid," she murmured slowly. "I am not afraid of anything with your arms round me, my desert lover. Ahmed! *Monseigneur!*"

ABOUT THE EDITOR

BARBARA CARTLAND, the celebrated romantic author, historian, playwright, lecturer, political speaker and television personality, has now written over 150 books. Miss Cartland has had a number of historical books published and several biographical ones, including that of her brother, Major Ronald Cartland, who was the first Member of Parliament to be killed in the War. This book had a Foreword by Sir Winston Churchill.

In private life, Barbara Cartland, who is a Dame of the Order of St. John of Jerusalem, has fought for better conditions and salaries for Midwives and Nurses. As President of the Royal College of Midwives (Hertfordshire Branch), she has been invested with the first Badge of Office ever given in Great Britain, which was subscribed to by the Midwives themselves. She has also championed the cause for old people and founded the first Romany Gypsy Camp in the world.

Barbara Cartland is deeply interested in Vitamin Therapy and is President of the British National Association for Health.

Barbara Cartland

The world's bestselling author of romantic fiction. Her stories are always captivating tales of intrigue, adventure and love.

☐	THE CRUEL COUNT	2128	$1.25
☐	CALL OF THE HEART	2140	$1.25
☐	AS EAGLES FLY	2147	$1.25
☐	THE MASK OF LOVE	2366	$1.25
☐	AN ARROW OF LOVE	2426	$1.25
☐	A GAMBLE WITH HEARTS	2430	$1.25
☐	A KISS FOR THE KING	2433	$1.25
☐	A FRAME OF DREAMS	2434	$1.25
☐	THE FRAGRANT FLOWER	2435	$1.25
☐	MOON OVER EDEN	2437	$1.25
☐	THE GOLDEN ILLUSION	2449	$1.25
☐	FIRE ON THE SNOW	2450	$1.25
☐	THE HUSBAND HUNTERS	2461	$1.25
☐	THE SHADOW OF SIN	6430	$1.25
☐	SAY YES, SAMANTHA	7834	$1.25
☐	THE KARMA OF LOVE	8106	$1.25
☐	BEWITCHED	8630	$1.25
☐	THE IMPETUOUS DUCHESS	8705	$1.25

Buy them at your local bookseller or use this handy coupon: